I0762780

Gödel and the Incomplete Proof

SAMUEL E. NAVARRO

GÖDEL AND THE INCOMPLETE PROOF

Conversations on Truth, Mystery, and the Answers Beyond Reason

amplify

www.amplifypublishinggroup.com

Gödel and the Incomplete Proof: Conversations on Truth, Mystery, and the Answers Beyond Reason

For more information, please contact:
Amplify Publishing, an imprint of Amplify Publishing Group
620 Herndon Parkway, Suite 220
Herndon, VA 20170
info@amplifypublishing.com

Library of Congress Control Number: 2025926198

CPSIA Code: PRV0126A

ISBN-13: 979-8-89138-958-8

Printed in the United States

With deepest gratitude to God, whose grace has guided every stop of this journey.

To my family—my greatest source of strength and joy.

To my wife, Alexandra, whose unwavering support and boundless love have given me the freedom to explore my dreams and the courage to follow my own path.

You have stood by me through every twist and turn, and I am forever grateful for that.

To my children and grandchildren, whose presence fills every journey with meaning and purpose. You are part of the reason I walk these paths with conviction, and you make every step truly worthwhile.

Now faith is the assurance of things hoped for, the conviction of things not seen.

—HEBREWS 11:1 (ESV)

For we walk by faith, not by sight.

—2 CORINTHIANS 5:7 (ESV)

CONTENTS

PREFACE

THE INCOMPLETE PROOF

Certainty is the comfort of those unwilling to think.

—SAMUEL E. NAVARRO

I've been wanting to write this book for years.

Not because I have the answers but because I've never been able to stop asking the questions.

These are the kind of questions that most people outgrow—or bury. The kind that show up late at night when the noise dies down. The ones that tug at the edges of logic and make you feel like a child again.

What is truth? Why does beauty pierce us? Is meaning something we invent—or something we uncover? Can reason ever explain love?

I've always found myself drawn to the thresholds—the places where knowledge ends and wonder begins. Where the map runs out. Where a model or a number no longer explains what's in front of you. Where the mind must kneel just to keep going.

It began not with Gödel but with a sense—a quiet but growing sense—that the world didn't work the way we were told. That behind the systems we build, the numbers we trust, and the truths we defend, there is silence. Not the silence of ignorance but the silence of something deeper: mystery. That we require more than what is provable yet knowable.

I studied engineering at the University of Texas at Austin, then went to Stanford University for graduate school. I did not finish my PhD, as I preferred to go into practice. I spent years designing structures meant to withstand earthquakes—elegant models bound by physical law, exact equations, and certainty—old-fashioned computational logic. Eventually, I moved to the East Coast, earning an MBA at the Wharton School and entering the machinery of New York City Wall Street. On to investment analysis, then investment banking. Then, on to hedge fund investment management and, eventually, a deep desire to step aside and think.

After five months of voracious reading and self-examination, a tempting offer to reengage Wall Street with a deeper and nonconformist approach followed. Not satisfied—and now better able to discern and withstand the pressures of groupthink—I decided to go on my own. Independence and controlling my own professional destiny ranked much higher than just money. I started a mergers and acquisitions boutique to pursue the dual goals of financial gains with a high degree of freedom to do what I wanted.

Over the years, I have seen and experienced the imprecision of markets and the madness of crowds. I saw how knowledge is traded like currency and how quickly consensus is confused with truth. I saw the shallowness of the masses' race to nowhere.

Through it all, I kept asking the oldest question of a rational mind: Why do we believe what we believe? Can we prove what we believe? This is old-fashioned epistemology. In my spare time, I delved into the history of philosophy, theology, doctrine, and practical logic.

I realized most people don't have the time or don't care to ask the big questions in life. Their beliefs, or lack of them, are inherited from their education, their environment, their careers, their social media, their fragmented news feeds, or their sad compromises made to avoid debate or not being liked or worse, risking their professional careers—as if there are no life consequences to avoiding the big questions of life. I couldn't shake the feeling that different domains of knowledge speak different languages—and sometimes, if we're honest, they contradict each other. Finance doesn't speak the way epistemology does. And physics doesn't speak the way the soul does. Sometimes, the heart and the mind disagree.

That's when Gödel found me.

His incompleteness theorems shook the foundations we thought were rock solid. Imagine you've built a clever little machine that can do basic arithmetic and prove any true statement about numbers—addition, multiplication, you name it. You'd expect it could answer every question you throw at it. But Gödel found a surprise hiding in the workings: In any system that's powerful enough to talk about arithmetic, there will always be true statements that the system can never prove.

Think of a formal system as a rules-based game: You begin with only a handful of axioms—your unshakable starting truths, like two plus two equals four—and a set of rules of inference, which are the cheat codes that let you build new truths from old ones.

Picture a game in which the axioms are the cards in your hand, and inference rules are the moves you can make to turn basic plays into dazzling combos. If the game is consistent, you'll never win and lose simultaneously—no statement and its exact opposite can sneak in. If it's complete, every possible move you can describe is either a clear win or a clear loss—there's no "maybe" or "undecided" on the scoreboard. Gödel's brilliant twist shows us that in any game rich enough to talk about arithmetic, there will always be a play so clever that the rules themselves can't prove whether it's a win or a loss.

Think of it like a phone book that claims to list every phone number in town. If the book is consistent, it won't list two different numbers for the same person. If it's complete, it will list every single valid number. Gödel's insight tells us this perfect phone book can't exist; you can't have both perfect consistency and perfect completeness. There will always be a number that really belongs in the book but isn't there—no matter how well you organize it, you'll miss something.

What does this mean? It means that no matter how elegant or airtight our logical systems are, they'll never capture every truth. There will always be a horizon just out of reach. Logic can guide us far but can't map the entire landscape.

Leibniz had dreamed of developing a "calculus of reason" where disputes could be settled by calculation. Gottfried Wilhelm Leibniz (1646–1716) was a German mathematician, philosopher, and statesman—born in Leipzig, later working across Europe and at the court of Hanover—who co-invented calculus with Newton and championed binary arithmetic. He dreamed of a "calculus of reason," a universal logical language plus simple, mechanical rules that would let people settle arguments the way we add numbers. In plain terms, if we could agree on a few basic starting truths and clear rules for combining them, questions in science, law, or even theology might be decided by calculation rather than quarrel.

Then came Gödel. He showed how to encode arithmetic in

symbols, and in doing so, he discovered the surprising limits of any such system. If, in any dispute, people agree, first, on a fixed set of starting truths (*axioms*) and exact rules for turning those truths into new ones (*inference rules*), then any domain of knowledge can be attempted to be formalized.

If you could force any dispute or domain of knowledge into a Gödel-style formal system, incompleteness would follow. The challenge is to turn them into rigid symbols that minimize or eliminate ambiguity without losing meaning.

Conclusively, incompleteness is universal. If we build a fully formal, unambiguous system that includes arithmetic, then Gödel guarantees there will be true but unprovable statements. If you leave your system vague—so you can preserve meaning—then you never had the airtight, symbol-only definitions Gödel needs to do his proof. Once you have enough precision to do a real calculation (axioms, no logical contradiction, and potential self-reference), you automatically invite Gödel's incompleteness.

Therefore, I would argue that every domain of knowledge can be attempted to be formalized. The arguments against that proposition include the following: Words carry connotations shaped by history and culture (different worldviews); context and metaphor are vital (such as disagreeing what grace means in one tradition versus another); and personal experience can shift a statement's resonance (bias). Yet, worldviews are necessarily full of axioms, which can be turned into symbolic logic, thereby allowing for precision in the proposition yet leaving open the possibility of disagreement without eliminating Gödel's high likelihood of incompleteness.

I wrote this book to explore that idea—not by lecturing but by imagining the ripple effects of Gödel's discovery far beyond number theory. What if Gödel, beyond the grave, could join conversations with some of history's greatest thinkers—not just mathematicians but scientists, philosophers, theologians, musicians, poets, and mystics? What if he could ask the questions he never finished: Can uncertainty principles go beyond math and forge doubts, like unprovable axioms that can impact and shape our moral frameworks? Can the limits of proof touch matters of faith, beauty, or purpose?

In this imaginative book, Gödel meets with many famous people in these fictional dialogues and travels through realms of meaning and arithmetic. They discuss not only equations and paradoxes but also suffering, grace, and the search for truth in many domains of knowledge. Each chapter is a step deeper into a grand labyrinth, not to escape complexity but to reveal how every field of knowledge shares the same horizon where certainty meets mystery.

I aim not to provide answers but to awaken questions—the kind of questions you don't shake off easily. I believe we don't meditate enough. And by meditating, I don't mean emptying the mind. I mean filling it—with wonder, paradox, and the joy of not knowing yet choosing. Because life is not a formula to be solved—it's a field of choices to be made.

And to choose well is not merely to follow instinct or yield to desire. It is to think with the heart and feel with the mind. To hold wisdom and freedom in the same breath. We are not animals bound by appetite nor machines governed by code. We are moral beings, made to navigate mystery—not with certainty but with conscience.

This book is an invitation to think critically, resist conformity, and rediscover the ancient art of asking. If you've ever felt that reason alone is not enough—that behind logic, there is music; behind order, there is awe—then this book is for you.

Because some truths cannot be proven, but they can be known.

And they are worth everything.

INTRODUCTION

GAPS IN THE SYSTEM

This statement is not provable.

—KURT GÖDEL

If you replace every part of a ship, is it still the same ship?

—PLUTARCH

What I do not know, I do not think I know.

—SOCRATES

THERE ARE QUESTIONS SO LARGE they cannot be held by the mind alone. They hang in the air like constellations—always above us, always pointing somewhere else. Every civilization has seen them. Every generation has named them: What is real? Why are we here? What is good? Where are we going?

This book begins with one such question—not answered, but reframed by a man whose discoveries changed everything, even if the world hasn't fully realized it yet.

His name was Kurt Gödel.

Brilliant, eccentric, unsettlingly precise—Gödel was not the kind of thinker who sought the spotlight. And yet, in the early twentieth century, this quiet logician rewrote the boundaries of human thought. He proved, in the most rigorous manner, that no formal system—no structure of logic or mathematics, regardless of how perfect—could be both complete and consistent. There would always be truths that were real but unprovable within the system itself.

In a world that had come to worship certainty, Gödel introduced mystery.

Not as an error. But as design. A mathematical proof for the unprovability of any formal system of knowledge.

His incompleteness theorems, published in 1931 at the tender age of twenty-four, were like a philosophical earthquake—shaking the foundations of mathematics, logic, and epistemology. But strangely, outside the world of academic logic, Gödel's work didn't filter into society the way Darwin's theory of evolution or Einstein's relativity did. No "Gödelian revolution" ever made its way into everyday speech. No cultural movement was named after him. No headlines. No public awakening.

And yet, his implications are deeper still. Where Darwin touched biology, and Einstein reshaped space and time, Gödel reached beyond both—to the very frame through which we see reality. He didn't just prove something about math. He exposed the limits of every human system of knowledge.

Why, then, have so few heard of him?

One of the provocations of this book is that Gödel's theorems didn't just shift a paradigm—they fractured the hope that any paradigm could hold all truth. Perhaps we didn't know what to do with that.

MR. WHY

He was called "Mr. Why" as a boy—Herr Warum—always asking questions no one else thought to ask. As he grew, his questions only deepened. What is the soul? What is time? Can mathematics capture meaning? Can reason lead us to God?

He wasn't content with technical brilliance. He sought metaphysical truth. Unlike many scientists of his era, Gödel believed in the soul and the afterlife. He believed that the mind was more than a machine and that intuition could reach truths that logic could only circle around.

In a world drifting into materialism, Gödel held fast to the idea that reality is not less than it appears but more—that the unseen is no less real than the measurable.

He died in Princeton in 1978, paranoid and emaciated—refusing to eat after his wife was hospitalized. And yet, even in his decline, the ideas he left behind grew in power, waiting to be unleashed again. Like J. S. Bach's music, rediscovered decades after his death, Gödel's theorems await his rediscovery and an appreciation of his grand consequences. His theorems became like mirrors, reflecting not just the structure of knowledge but the mystery at its core.

CONVERSATIONS BEYOND CERTAINTY AND TIME

This book is a collection of **imagined dialogues** between Gödel and some of the greatest minds in history—philosophers, scientists, theologians, musicians, and poets of logic and form. These are not biographical reconstructions. They are metaphysical encounters, parables of thought, fictional but faithful to the ideas each thinker represents.

What would Gödel say to a pioneer of science who insisted everything must be testable?

What might he hear from a philosopher who believed reason could map the limits of itself?

Could he find harmony with a composer whose music seemed to gesture toward the eternal?

Would he challenge those who placed their faith entirely in reason—or echo it in a deeper key?

Some of these thinkers will challenge Gödel, and others will agree with him. Some will question the limits of provability. Others will press the question of falsifiability, as Karl Popper once did, arguing that while nothing can be proven with certainty, everything must be testable to be believed. But what—Gödel might ask—do we do with the truths that are testable in no laboratory, repeatable in no experiment—like beauty, justice, meaning, or love?

These dialogues are woven with irony, faith, paradox, even speculation, and the persistent tug of mystery.

They take place in strange and timeless places: beneath golden arches, in candlelit sanctuaries, across the dusty stone of ancient temples, and in the bright logic of future laboratories. Gödel walks these spaces with quiet intensity, not to debate but to listen, to wonder, and to ask again, "Why?"

THE FABRIC OF REALITY . . . AND ITS SEAMS

We live in an age obsessed with certainty yet haunted by mystery. We know more than ever—and understand less. Science explains the how but often stumbles at the why. Philosophy dares to ask what is real but fractures under the weight of competing worldviews. Technology connects us instantly—yet leaves us longing for depth.

Gödel's work invites us to pause.

To return to the basic fact that knowledge has boundaries. That there are seams in the fabric of reality. And that these seams are not failures—they are the places where something greater shines through.

He reminds us that there are truths that we believe not because we can prove them but because we must believe them. They are axioms of life—like that love is essential to human well-being, that justice is the foundation of a moral society, and that beauty is more than preference—it points beyond itself to a deeper reality.

Faith, in this frame, is not the enemy of logic. It is its companion at the edge.

Again, Popper—who challenged the entire philosophy of scientific proof—acknowledged that absolute certainty is elusive. His method of falsification wasn't about proving what is true but about testing what can survive disproof. And yet, even this system collapses when we ask: Can the deepest truths—personal, moral, spiritual—be falsified?

And if not, are they less real? Or more?

WHAT THIS BOOK HOPES TO DO

This book doesn't offer answers. It offers encounters. It invites you to listen in as Gödel walks through centuries of human thought—stirring, unsettling, revealing.

It hopes to awaken two longings in you:

First, to see Gödel not as a cold mathematician but as a philosopher of mystery—one who helps us understand why truth will always be more than what we can prove.

Second, to question the sufficiency of materialism and to rediscover a hunger for the infinite—for wonder, faith, and the logic of what cannot be reduced.

From the paradoxes of quantum mechanics to the beauty of fractals, from the burden of wisdom to the silence of God, these dialogues reach across disciplines—not to solve everything but to stir within you the desire to keep asking.

Gödel showed that even the most solid structures—mathematics, logic, science—rest on foundations that cannot be proven from within. The same may be true of life. Our stories, our values, our hopes—all of them may be built on truths that cannot be verified but only believed.

And that is the greatest proof of all.

Faith, in this light, is not a retreat from knowledge—it is the threshold of it. The ancients understood what many moderns have forgotten: that certainty is not the doorway to meaning but the hallway out of it. Augustine of Hippo said, "Believe so that you might understand," and Anselm echoed it centuries later—not as blind surrender but as recognition: that some truths can only be seen once the eyes of the soul are open.

It is not *understanding* that produces *faith.*

It is *faith* that makes *understanding possible.*

Like Gödel himself, this book stands in the space between what we can prove and what we must receive. It is not an argument to win but a journey to take—a reawakening of wonder, a return to mystery, a quiet echo of something eternal.

So come walk with Gödel. Step into the questions that echo across time. Stand beneath the stars. Let wonder return.

Let the limits of human knowledge become the doorway to something more.

Let the journey begin.

SECTION I

LOGIC, MATH, AND SCIENCE

CHAPTER ONE

THE MACHINE THAT COULDN'T KNOW

—von Neumann

Singular and monumental—indeed it is more than a monument; it is a landmark which will remain visible far in space and time. The subject of logic will never again be the same.

—JOHN VON NEUMANN (referring to Gödel's incompleteness theorems)

In a dim corner of the Princeton University library, surrounded by towering shelves filled with centuries of accumulated knowledge, Kurt Gödel sat alone. He was hunched over a stack of books, intently scribbling notes on a small notepad, utterly absorbed in the symphony of symbols and formulas that filled his mind. Gödel had an almost spectral quality—thin, with a distant look in his eyes and a demeanor that seemed to make the air around him dense and still. Most students and professors alike knew to avoid disturbing him. He was not just another academic; he was Kurt Gödel, a man whose intellect had already cast a formidable shadow over the mathematical landscape.

The Princeton library itself was as storied as the institution. Built on the principles of quietude and learning, it held endless shelves of rare manuscripts and monographs, each aisle a solemn testament to humankind's quest for understanding. Dust particles floated lazily in beams of light, catching the silence like ancient secrets. The scent of old leather and parchment filled the space, a comforting smell for those who found refuge in the world of ideas.

Outside, winter had laid its quiet claim over Princeton, cloaking the university grounds in snow that softened the edges of every building and muffled the usual campus bustle. The evening air was frigid, biting at the few who hurried past the library's frosted windows. Inside, Gödel barely noticed the deepening chill or the late hour, utterly lost in his work. The thought of dinner had long since slipped his mind; to him, time passed like the turning of pages—irrelevant, merely a detail in the background of his thoughts. For Gödel, who often lived in the abstractions of his mind, the encroaching night and icy winds were little more than whispers beyond the fortress of his solitude.

Gödel's corner was far from any entrances or exits, a secluded alcove where he could lose himself in thought without interruption. As he pored over a treatise on formal logic, his mind drifted between concepts, weaving thoughts on completeness, provability, and the nature of mathematical truth. He had once captivated the world with these very ideas. In 1931, at the age of twenty-four, Gödel had attended a Vienna conference and presented a discovery that shook the foundation of mathematics itself: his incompleteness theorems. In essence, Gödel had shown that within any consistent mathematical system, there would always be true statements that could not be proven within that system. The revelation stunned the audience—mathematicians, logicians, and philosophers alike. The notion that not all truths were provable was, for many, a seismic shift in how they understood not just mathematics but knowledge itself.

What Gödel achieved in 1931 wasn't speculation or philosophical conjecture. Gödel had written his theorems in the precise language of mathematics itself. Mathematics, the most rigorous and exact of disciplines, left no room for guesswork or subjective interpretation. His proofs were pure logic, tested by symbols and equations, a step-by-step dismantling of assumptions. Mathematics is often seen as the language of certainty, the one field where truth feels concrete, where ideas can be pinned down with accuracy. Yet Gödel had used this very language to demonstrate the existence of truths that lay beyond proof, showing the world that even in mathematics, not everything could be neatly contained. This was not merely an opinion but a mathematical certainty, a revelation that echoed far beyond formulas and equations, calling into question the foundations of logical understanding.

For decades, intellectuals in the fields of logic and mathematics, such as Bertrand Russell, Alfred North Whitehead, and David Hilbert (all members of the Vienna Circle), had sought to ground mathematics using symbolic logic. It was called Logical Positivism—essentially stating that the only meaningful philosophical problems are those that can be solved by logical analysis. They aimed to eliminate paradoxes or contradictions that seem to make no sense. Gödel's 1931 presentation obliterated the hopes of these intellectuals and many other prodigies of establishing a complete and consistent set of axioms for all mathematics through formal systems. What Gödel showed was that not all mathematical truths can be derived from logical axioms alone. His incompleteness theorems shattered the dream of proving all mathematical truths, as if the rug was being pulled out from under mathematics.

It was now the 1940s, and Gödel sat immersed in the university library, absorbed in the realm of physics and philosophy. Perched on a sturdy, richly stained wooden chair, he seemed captivated by the drive to unearth new knowledge. Just then, a faint rustling from the adjacent aisle signaled another presence. John von Neumann had not expected to see Gödel here in the library. Von Neumann was a Hungarian-born mathematician, physicist, computer scientist, and engineer. In 1909, at six years old, von Neumann could divide two eight-digit numbers in his head and hold a conversation in ancient Greek.

Von Neumann was one of the most influential minds of his generation. A polymath who seamlessly moved between pure mathematics, physics, and the emerging field of computer science, his work laid the groundwork for digital computing, game theory, and even atomic research. Known for his brilliance and confidence, he had a presence that commanded attention even in a silent library.

Von Neumann's contributions to game theory sparked a revolution in understanding strategic decision-making. His groundbreaking work, *Theory of Games and Economic Behavior* (1944), laid the foundation for what would become Nash equilibrium theory. Years later, John Nash would stand on von Neumann's shoulders, refining the ideas of competition and strategy into a theory that could predict the behavior of multiple rational actors in situations of conflict or cooperation. Where von Neumann had envisioned game theory as a tool for war and economics, Nash saw it as a key to social dynamics, personal rivalries, and even everyday choices. In ways von Neumann never imagined, his ideas became the backbone of modern economics, political science, and behavioral analysis—a legacy that proved just as consequential as his advances in computing and logic.

Noticing Gödel out of the corner of his eye, von Neumann hesitated. He respected Gödel's solitude but was genuinely curious. Their paths had crossed often at Princeton's Institute for Advanced Study, yet he had rarely had the chance to speak with Gödel one-on-one. The only close intellectual companion of Gödel at Princeton's Institute for Advanced Studies was Albert Einstein. They often walked home together from the institute, engaging in deep conversations.

Intrigued upon seeing Gödel, von Neuman walked over quietly, hoping not to intrude. "Kurt," he whispered with a faint smile, "I didn't expect to find you here." Gödel looked up, momentarily startled. He blinked twice, recognition slowly settling in, and then offered a slight nod. Von Neumann's presence was not entirely unwelcome—if anyone understood the weight of his ideas, it would be von Neumann.

"John," Gödel replied softly, his tone neutral, as though he were adjusting to the idea of the company. "It's . . . rare to see you in the library as well."

Von Neumann chuckled, glancing at the surrounding shelves. "I suppose even I can't resist the lure of all this knowledge," he said, gesturing broadly. "Though I doubt I'd make as much sense of it as you do."

For a moment, they stood in silence, each man appreciating the other's achievements and intellect. Von Neumann knew about Gödel's 1931 presentation and often pondered its implications. The incompleteness theorems represented something fundamentally unsettling yet oddly beautiful, a reminder of the limits within even the purest form of logic.

Von Neumann broke the silence. "I've been meaning to ask you about Vienna and your presentation there. You really shook the world with that one, Kurt."

Gödel allowed a faint smile to cross his face, the memory of that conference both vivid and haunting. "I suppose I only proved what I already suspected—that mathematics, like so much else, is limited by its own framework."

Von Neumann's eyes lit up. "But it's not just mathematics, is it?" he said, pressing gently. "Your theorems imply a boundary, a kind of horizon beyond which we can't see. That must have been hard for people to accept, even dangerous."

Figure 1. One of the earliest electronic computers (ENIAC) at Aberdeen Proving Ground, Maryland (between 1947-1955). Source: M. Weik, US Army, via Wikimedia Commons (public domain).

For many, especially secular scientists, anything suggesting limits on human knowledge or hinting at the mysterious is unsettling. Modern science prides itself on unraveling mysteries, shining light into every corner of the unknown. Faith, in any form, can seem like an unscientific surrender to the unexplainable. Yet Gödel's work had introduced an unresolvable mystery into the very heart of logic. It challenged a worldview that believed all things could be understood with enough time and reason, forcing the scientific world to confront an unsettling truth: that logic itself could harbor mysteries. For some, this notion felt too close to faith—a recognition that some aspects of reality might forever remain beyond reach, inviting wonder and humility in a field defined by certainty.

Gödel nodded, acknowledging the weight of his ideas. "It was . . . unexpected," he admitted. "And unsettling. For those of us who believed that mathematics could be complete, consistent, and certain, it was an uncomfortable revelation."

Von Neumann knew he was hinting at David Hilbert. Hilbert had spent his life building a vision of mathematics as a perfectly logical structure—a unified, complete system. His famous "Hilbert's Program" aimed to establish mathematics as a field where every truth could be rigorously proven. The very premise of Gödel's work had toppled Hilbert's vision, and von Neumann could only imagine the shock it caused. Gödel's findings had rendered Hilbert's lifelong ambition, in a sense, unreachable. It was as if an explorer had mapped every detail of an unknown land, only to find an unbridgeable chasm lying in its center.

Sensing that von Neumann wanted to understand more deeply, Gödel decided to offer a more approachable explanation. "Think of it this way, John," he began. "Imagine a book of truths, every page filled with statements about our world. If you keep reading, you'll find that for every truth you encounter, there's a question about that truth the book can't answer. It's like . . . a treasure chest that won't open unless you already know what's inside."

Von Neumann, always quick to understand analogies, nodded. "So, the system itself can't unlock everything about itself?"

"Exactly," Gödel replied, warming to the discussion. "Now imagine we built a machine to answer every question in that book. But that machine would inevitably hit a question that it couldn't answer about itself, like a riddle it can't solve because it's part of the riddle. And that's what I found in mathematics: Some questions are simply unanswerable, but they're not meaningless. They're just . . . beyond the machine's reach."

Von Neumann raised an eyebrow. "Then the chest is only truly valuable if we have faith before—faith, before the fact—that its contents are worth seeking. And yet, for that faith to mean anything, it must be a logical faith, something that makes sense based on what we already know, even if we can't open the chest entirely."

Gödel nodded, a slight smile on his lips. "Yes, John. Faith isn't about accepting the illogical or abandoning reason. It's about reaching for truths that are beyond proof but not beyond understanding. Just because something lies outside our system doesn't mean it's unreasonable. It may be unseen, but it must be built on sound principles, logical yet unprovable within the system itself."

Von Neumann considered this. Gödel's analogy resonated, hinting at faith in unseen truths not based on blind acceptance but on the logical foundation of everything known so far. Gödel's quiet belief in something beyond mathematics, a transcendent logic, gave von Neumann pause. It was as if Gödel was suggesting that faith, at its core, was a logical extension of human understanding—something founded on the rational yet reaching into the unprovable.

Gödel, known for his private spiritual leanings, saw this transcendence not as a failing but as a hint at something greater. Although he rarely spoke openly about his beliefs, he saw his discoveries as part of a world governed by truths beyond human reach—a reality more intricate than logic alone could define. It is conjectured that he once said in responding to the Vienna Circle, "If there were no higher beings with an absolute perception of truth, then all our efforts to learn and know would indeed be vain."

The Vienna Circle was a group of philosophers, scientists, and mathematicians who met regularly in Vienna during the 1920s and 1930s. Their goal was to make philosophy as precise and scientific as possible. They believed that only statements that can be directly verified through experience, or that can be logically proven (like in math), are meaningful. If a claim couldn't be checked with evidence or logic, they thought it was nonsense. The group was known for "logical positivism" (also called "logical empiricism").

Gödel lived with an inclination toward theism. In essence, Gödel believed in the existence of absolute truths that were independent of human perception or formal systems. In fact, Gödel developed a formal, mathematical version of the ontological argument for the existence of God, an attempt to demonstrate the logical necessity of a supreme being. Gödel's ontological argument (1987) was not published until after his death (1978) but was a strong indication of his belief in a logically grounded theistic concept.

Von Neumann, more pragmatic yet equally fascinated, murmured, "It seems, Kurt, that even we, who have ventured so deeply into logic, must still face mysteries. We must still accept that there are things we can't fully know."

The room grew silent again, but this time, it was a peaceful silence, filled with the quiet awe of two minds resting in the presence of something unknown. They each recognized that at the heart of knowledge lay an unanswerable question, one that required, if nothing else, the humility to admit its existence. And perhaps, for Gödel, that humility had always been tied to faith—a belief that behind every mystery, there lay a truth, even if unseen.

As they left the library, Gödel turned to von Neumann with a slight, almost mischievous smile. "In the end, John, perhaps we are all searching for something we cannot prove but only sense. And maybe that is proof enough."

They walked away, knowing that although mathematics might have its limits, the pursuit of truth—through faith or reason—was boundless.

CHAPTER TWO

TRUTH ON TRIAL

—Popper

As our knowledge expands, our awareness of the limits of what we understand also grows.

—attributed to ARISTOTLE

The more we know, the more we realize how much we do not know.

—ALBERT EINSTEIN (echoing Aristotle)

THE PUB NEAR THE LONDON SCHOOL OF ECONOMICS (LSE) was alive with the hum of conversation and the clinking of beer mugs and coffee cups. The scent of lagers, dark coffee, and freshly baked pastries filled the air, a familiar comfort to Kurt Gödel as he adjusted his glasses and stirred his espresso. He had always enjoyed the intellectual vibrancy of London's pubs, where philosophers, scientists, and mathematicians had for generations debated the nature of truth.

The LSE itself was a significant gathering point for leading thinkers of the era. The school attracted economists, philosophers, scientists, and social reformers, often serving as a meeting ground for debates and discussions. Notably, in 1924, a meeting at the London School of Economics (LSE) led to the founding of the Royal Institute of Philosophy, with the explicit aim of making philosophical discussion accessible to the London public and involving a wide range of intellectuals from various disciplines.

As Gödel turned the pages of a worn philosophical treatise, a familiar voice called out.

"Gödel! What a surprise to see you here. May I join?"

Gödel looked up and saw Karl Popper standing before him, his characteristic sharp gaze scanning the table for an empty seat. Popper was not one for idle socializing; he engaged with people only when he saw intellectual purpose in doing so. Gödel nodded, gesturing to the seat across from him.

"Of course, Karl. I suspect you are not here merely for the coffee."

Popper smirked as he set his cup down. "Indeed not. But then again, neither are you."

Popper never merely entered a room; he colonized it. His greatcoat swung like a door unlatched, scattering dust motes that glittered in a late-evening-lit pub. To the few intellectuals who watched him stride past, Popper was already legendary: the refugee from Vienna who had dared to tell the scientific world it progresses not by confirming truths but by killing cherished ideas.

Karl Popper was born in 1902 on the edge of the Austro-Hungarian twilight. He apprenticed as a cabinetmaker, flirted with Marxism, and found his profession in demolishing overconfident theories. When Nazi pressure darkened Vienna in 1937, Popper escaped to New Zealand with nothing but manuscripts and a conviction that open societies survive by learning to doubt themselves. Eventually, he landed at the LSE in 1946, where his lectures were equal parts sermon and street fight—one moment gentle, the next a volley of questions that left even seasoned scholars breathless.

Gödel smiled. "Just looking for a little quiet."

"There is no quiet once an idea is born," Popper said, sliding confidently into the opposite chair. He pulled a battered notebook from his pocket. "Your incompleteness proofs kept me awake. Again."

"Insomnia," Gödel murmured, "is a faithful companion to anyone chasing certainty."

Popper sipped the contraband coffee, wincing at its strength. "Certainty is overrated. Give me a bold conjecture and a sharper test," Popper said. He flipped open the notebook. "Let us talk about how we know when a theory fails."

POPPER'S PRINCIPLE OF FALSIFICATION

Gödel nodded. "I am well aware of your views. You propose that instead of seeking ultimate verification, science should move forward by eliminating errors. By discarding what is false, we edge closer to truth. An admirable principle." Gödel added, "And yet, your principle assumes that within the domain of scientific knowledge, truth is always accessible—that by testing and refining, we eventually approach it. But what if some truths are beyond our capacity to verify or falsify? What if there are truths that, while logically sound, can never be proven or disproven within the system in which they are formulated?"

Popper, in his self-grandiose confidence, sketched a swan—white, theatrical—and then another, dark as coal. "For centuries, Europeans believed all swans were white. Then explorers reached Australia and—poof!—one black swan punctured the rule. A single counterexample can mow down a thousand confirmations."

Gödel folded his hands. "A vivid argument. Yet your swan is a bird, not a sentence. Formal systems behave differently."

"But the principle is the same," Popper insisted. "A claim that cannot be falsified belongs to metaphysics, not science."

Figure 2. Karl Popper (1990). Source: Wikimedia Commons (public domain).

Gödel leaned forward. "Karl, imagine a statement that cannot be falsified yet cannot be verified either because its very wording refers to the system judging it. Like a letter sealed inside an envelope that says, 'The statement in this envelope is unprovable.' Open it, and you face a paradox: Prove it, and you make it false; disprove it, and you confirm it."

Popper raised an eyebrow. "Your famous self-reference. But surely a scientist can ignore such trick sentences and press on with real-world tests."

"A mathematician once told me that," Gödel replied. "Then he tried to build a computer program to decide whether any program would ever halt. He discovered my hydra still breathes inside the circuits."

Popper drummed his fingers. "The halting problem?" Introduced in 1936 by Alan Turing, a British mathematician and logician, his work essentially stated that there is no general algorithm that can determine whether a computer program will halt (finish running) or run forever, given a specific input. The halting problem was acknowledged to be undecidable yet a cornerstone of computational science and software engineering. It demonstrated the fundamental limits of what can be computed.

"Exactly," Gödel responded. "A black swan made of germanium," hinting at the inherent limitations of Popper's groundbreaking thesis.

Popper sat back, his brow furrowing. "That is a dangerous road, Gödel. If we accept that some scientific truths cannot be tested, we risk opening the door to unfounded speculation. Science must remain empirical. It cannot be based on unprovable assumptions."

Gödel allowed a small smile. "And yet, Karl, you yourself rely on certain assumptions that you do not, and cannot, falsify."

Popper frowned. "Such as?"

Gödel gestured subtly. "Your entire principle of falsification. Have you ever falsified the principle of falsification itself? Can you?"

Popper opened his mouth to respond but hesitated. Gödel pressed further. "You assume that falsifiability is the criterion that separates science from nonscience, but that principle itself is not falsifiable. It is an axiom, a foundational belief about how knowledge should be structured. Just as my incompleteness theorems reveal that mathematics requires unprovable truths as its foundation, so too does your philosophy of science."

Popper's face tensed for a moment, but then he let out a small chuckle. "I see what you are doing, Gödel. You are using my own logic against me."

"Not against you," Gödel said softly. "With you. You argue that knowledge progresses through falsification, and I do not deny that. But what I add is that even falsification has its limits. Some truths—whether in mathematics or in nature—are simply beyond our reach, yet they still shape our understanding."

THE AGREEMENT

Popper leaned back, exhaling deeply. "So, you suggest that rather than absolute falsifiability, science—like mathematics—may rest upon assumptions that we must accept, even if we can never test them? So, my rule might be an instrument—a tool—rather than a theorem?"

"Nothing wrong with that," Gödel said. "But instruments, like axioms, stand outside the structures they help build."

Popper rubbed his temples, never before having been challenged this way. "Let me try an experiment. Find fields where progress happens without testable claims: Astrology makes no progress; psychoanalysis wanders—where is the advance? In contrast, testable theories like evolutionary biology thrive on risky predictions, physics too."

Gödel set down the cup. "You have switched to sociology: counting who prospers. That is persuasive, but not logical falsification. Your principle resembles a compass—useful for navigation, yet the compass needle cannot point to its own north." He was implying that the compass needle cannot inspect (prove) the magnet that guides it.

Gödel continued, "We must recognize that even our most rigorous methods of inquiry rest on foundations that, while reliable, may never be fully provable or falsifiable. That does not mean we abandon them—it means we acknowledge their nature. Yet we progress."

Popper responded nervously. "Still, an unfalsifiable compass feels like hypocrisy."

Gödel's eyes warmed. "Only if you confuse *guidance* with *guarantee*. My incompleteness theorem shows that no map, however large, can include a perfect copy of itself. Your falsification reminds us to keep redrawing the coastline. Together, they warn against hubris."

Popper stared at his coffee for a long moment, then laughed. "You have given me much to think about, Gödel. I came to challenge you, and yet you have made me question my own framework. I must thank you for that."

Gödel smiled. "The pursuit of truth is not a contest, Karl. It is an endless conversation."

Popper leaned in. "May I confess? When I first wrote *The Logic of Scientific Discovery* (1934), I believed I had finally grounded knowledge in rock. But every decade since, I've watched the ground slowly shift under my feet. New ways of doing science keep appearing, different schools of thought compete for dominance, and the rules of the game keep changing. What once felt certain now feels less secure, as if the very foundations of how we understand truth are always moving. Your theorems whisper, 'Foundations are quieter when they float.'"

Gödel spread his hands. "Floating is not falling. Think of Archimedes: A body sinks until it finds the density that bears it. Truth may be similar—part weight, part buoyancy."

"Touché," Popper said. He raised his cup. "To that, I can certainly drink."

The two men sat in quiet contemplation, sipping their coffee as the world around them carried on—oblivious to the seismic shift that had just occurred in the minds of two of the greatest thinkers of their age.

CHAPTER THREE

THE UNCERTAINTY OF KNOWING

—Schrödinger

I have no doubt that the universe is governed by laws, but these laws may still be incomplete.

– paraphrasing **ERWIN SCHRÖDINGER**

A COLD MIST LINGERED over Vienna's post-war old city as Kurt Gödel stepped into a quiet coffeehouse. The scent of dark roast and warm strudel wrapped around him like an old friend. He hesitated for a moment, adjusting his coat. Conversations were never easy for him—his mind worked in abstractions, in deep logic that often made ordinary social interactions feel unnecessary. But then, in the farthest corner, he spotted a familiar face: Erwin Schrödinger, hunched over a cup of Einspänner, absentmindedly stirring the whipped cream into his coffee.

Gödel approached cautiously. "Erwin," he said softly, "I didn't expect to see you here. May I join?"

Schrödinger looked up, blinking as if pulled from another world. Then, a slow, amused smile formed on his lips. "Kurt! Of course! No need for formalities. We're both creatures of thought, wandering in and out of our own minds. Sit."

Gödel slid into the seat, glancing at the pile of papers beside Schrödinger. "Still pondering the mysteries of the universe?"

Schrödinger chuckled. "Always. These days, it seems the universe plays more tricks on us than we play on it. For instance, my cat."

THE CAT THAT WOULDN'T DIE (OR WOULD IT?)

Gödel raised an eyebrow. "Ah, yes, the famous cat. I was just thinking about that."

Schrödinger sighed. "It was supposed to be a thought experiment. A way to show how ridiculous quantum mechanics sounds when applied to the real world. But now, people talk about the cat as if it was a real experiment. I should have chosen a goldfish."

Gödel smirked. "A goldfish wouldn't have the same dramatic effect."

Schrödinger leaned forward, his hands wrapped around his coffee cup. "Imagine this: You have a cat inside a box. Along with it, there's a vial of poison and a tiny bit of radioactive material. The way quantum mechanics works, we can't know for sure whether the radioactive material has decayed until we check. If it decays, it triggers a mechanism that breaks the vial, releasing poison. If it hasn't decayed, the cat is safe."

Gödel nodded. "But until you open the box, the cat exists in a strange state—both dead and alive."

"Exactly!" Schrödinger said. "In classical physics, things have definite states. A light switch is either on or off, your coffee is either hot or cold. But in quantum mechanics, particles exist in a 'superposition'—they are in multiple states at once until we measure them. When we observe, the system 'chooses' an outcome."

"But what does that mean?" Gödel asked, leaning in. "Is the cat truly in both states, or does it just appear that way to us?"

Figure 3. Schrödinger (circled, center top) at the Solvay Conference, 1927, alongside his contemporaries—Einstein, Bohr, Heisenberg, and others—at the seminal meeting where quantum theory debates peaked. Source: Benjamin Couprie / Institut International de Physique Solvay, via Wikimedia Commons (public domain).

Schrödinger exhaled, rubbing his temple. "That's the troubling part. The Copenhagen interpretation, which many physicists accept, suggests that reality itself does not settle on an outcome until it is observed. Imagine flipping a coin, but instead of it landing on heads or tails, it remains suspended in both possibilities until you glance at it. Only when you look does it 'decide' which side it landed on."

"That would make reality . . . contingent on observation," Gödel said slowly. "Which means the moon does not exist if no one looks at it?"

Schrödinger shrugged. "Einstein certainly hated that idea. 'God does not play dice,' he said. And yet, experiments confirm that at the smallest scales, particles behave exactly as if they are in multiple states until measured."

GÖDEL'S INCOMPLETENESS AND THE NATURE OF TRUTH

Gödel's eyes brightened. "That reminds me of something. My incompleteness theorems suggest that in any logical system, there are truths that can never be proven within the system itself. No matter how much we try to explain everything, there will always be some truths just out of reach."

Schrödinger tilted his head. "And you think the same applies to physics?"

"I suspect so," Gödel said. "What if there are aspects of reality—things we desperately want to know—that are fundamentally unknowable? Not just because we don't have the right tools, but because they are beyond the limits of any possible knowledge?"

Schrödinger stirred his coffee. "So, you're saying there might never be a grand unifying equation of everything? No single formula that explains it all?"

Gödel smiled. "Wouldn't that be fitting? That reality itself is built with uncertainty woven into its very fabric?"

Schrödinger exhaled, thinking. "If you're right, then it's not just physics that's incomplete—it's everything. Perhaps we have to accept that mystery is part of the design."

FROM QUANTUM STATES TO QUANTUM COMPUTING

Schrödinger took another sip of his coffee. "You know, I keep thinking about how we can use this uncertainty instead of fighting it. What if we don't force things to collapse into one state but instead embrace their multiple possibilities?"

Gödel raised an eyebrow. "What do you mean?"

"Quantum computing," Schrödinger said. "Right now, traditional computers process information using bits—each bit is either zero or one. But in a quantum computer, bits, called 'qubits,' can be both zero and one at the same time. It's like flipping a coin, but instead of waiting for it to land heads or tails, it stays in the air, existing as both. This means quantum computers could process enormous amounts of information at once."

Gödel's expression darkened slightly. "But will we ever truly understand it? Or is it just another tool we use without fully grasping its meaning?"

Schrödinger laughed. "Does it matter? People don't fully understand how electronic communications work, but they still use them every day. Maybe the quest for knowledge isn't about finding an endpoint but learning how to work with the unknown."

THE LIMITS OF KNOWING

Gödel nodded. "Imagine a vast horizon—every theorem we prove, every equation we solve extends our reach, but the horizon itself always moves further away, like living Zeno's paradox. Perhaps reality is structured this way intentionally. If everything could be known, would there be anything left worth seeking?"

Schrödinger tilted his head. "You almost make it sound like a design. Does that imply a designer? That there's something infinite out there, just beyond what we can ever fully grasp?"

Gödel smirked. "It's certainly possible. But whether there is a designer, the duality and uncertainty of the universe remind us of our own limits. And perhaps that's not a flaw—it's an invitation to keep exploring."

Schrödinger raised his Einspänner cup. "To paradoxes, limitations, and the wonderful, incomprehensible universe."

Gödel lifted his glass of warm milk. "To the cat—wherever it may be, dead or alive."

And as the bells of Saint Stephen's Cathedral rang in the distance, the two great minds sat together, content in the knowledge that some mysteries would always remain just out of reach, waiting to be pondered over coffee.

CHAPTER FOUR

THE HIDDEN SEQUENCE

—Fibonacci

Some of the greatest mathematical minds of all ages . . . have spent endless hours over this simple ratio and its properties. But the fascination with the golden ratio is not confined just to mathematicians . . . In fact, it is probably fair to say that the golden ratio has inspired thinkers of all disciplines like no other number in the history of mathematics.

—MARIO LIVIO

KURT GÖDEL DRIFTED into a strange sleep, the kind that felt neither entirely dream nor entirely reality. He was standing in a sun-drenched courtyard, the air thick with the scent of oranges and sea spray. The stone walls were ancient, covered in climbing vines that coiled in perfect spirals. A marble fountain appeared softly in the center, its water rippling outward in golden proportions—it had to be Italian Romanesque or early Gothic architecture. Gödel blinked in confusion—he had never been here before, yet something about it felt . . . inevitable. It was the time the now-famous Tower of Pisa started to come together, a wonder of the human mind and human execution.

As the sun's warm embrace settled into his coat, lending it a subtle, weighted texture, he lifted his gaze. And then he saw him.

A man dressed in the simple robes of a thirteenth-century scholar sat under an olive tree, scribbling in a parchment notebook. His face seemed to have been weathered by the Mediterranean sun, his eyes alight with the kind of curiosity that never fades, not even after centuries. The scholar looked up from his work, studying Gödel with an expression that was neither startled nor unwelcoming. He was inherently a wonderer of mysteries.

"You look lost, traveler," the man said in a fluid Italian accent, his quill pausing above the parchment. The man was, as if led by a strange instinct, driven to guess the faces and forms of strangers. "But perhaps you are not lost at all. Perhaps you have been led here by numbers."

Gödel felt a shiver at the words. "You . . . you are Fibonacci."

The man smiled. "I have been called many names, but yes, that is one of them. And you"—he tilted his head—"you are not from my time."

"No," Gödel admitted. "My name is Kurt Gödel. I come from a future where your numbers, your sequences, have taken on a life of their own. Your work extends beyond counting rabbits, Maestro Fibonacci. You discovered something profound, something hidden within the very fabric of nature."

Fibonacci chuckled, tapping his parchment. "Ah, the rabbits! They were a mere beginning. A simple thought experiment, yet from it, a great pattern emerged." He gestured to his notes. "One pair of rabbits gives birth to another. In the next month, both pairs reproduce. The next, more join them. And so, it continues—each generation born from the sum of those before." He paused, looking at Gödel. "Tell me, in your time, do they still find this pattern in nature?"

Gödel nodded. "Everywhere. In the spirals of shells, in the branching of trees, in the unfurling of ferns. Even in galaxies, the very structure of the universe. And then, there is the golden ratio, hidden within your sequence, appearing in the proportions of flowers, in the symmetry of faces, in the way storms curl upon themselves. It is as though nature has written your numbers into its very design."

With a spark of wonder lighting his eyes, Fibonacci described to Gödel how he one day realized that what appeared as a simple recreational exercise had, in fact, unlocked a universal melody—a sequence that would forever resonate in the spiraled petals of flowers and the graceful unfurling of leaves. This led to the discovery of the golden ratio.

Fibonacci leaned back against the olive tree, a satisfied glint in his eyes. "I always suspected the numbers were not mine at all but something eternal, something merely waiting to be discovered. I am only an instrument of a . . . what can I say . . . a Grand Designer."

Gödel felt a deep resonance with those words. "Yes. That is the paradox of knowledge. We do not create truth—it is only revealed, bit by bit. And yet, I have discovered that mathematics, for all its beauty, has limits. Some truths exist that can never be proven within the system they belong to."

Fibonacci raised an eyebrow. "You mean to say that numbers themselves hold mysteries that even logic cannot fully grasp?"

"Yes," Gödel said with quiet intensity. "Just as your sequence stretches toward infinity, never reaching a final number, mathematical systems contain statements that, though true, can never be proven within their own framework. No matter how perfect the structure, something will always remain outside of it."

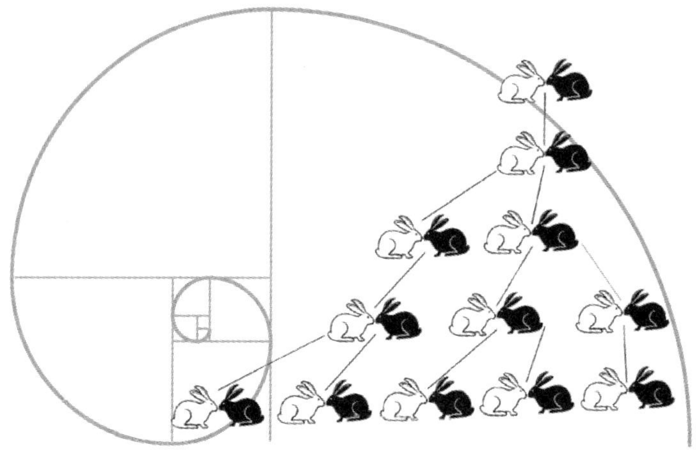

Figure 4. Schematic of paired rabbits as Fibonacci posed in *Liber Abaci*. Source: ETH Library, "The rabbit problem" (public domain).

Fibonacci stroked his beard, considering. "Then perhaps numbers are like the spiral of a shell—always curving outward, always leading somewhere new, but never closing in on themselves completely."

"Yes!" Gödel's heart pounded with recognition. "That is exactly it. Your spiral—the logarithmic spiral—expands infinitely, never reaching a final boundary. It is the same with knowledge. We build our theorems, we discover patterns, yet there will always be something beyond, something just outside our reach."

Fibonacci smiled knowingly. "And yet, does that not make the pursuit even more beautiful? If all could be known, where would be the wonder?"

Fibonacci leaned forward, tracing a number in the dust on the stone bench beside him—a single zero, its shape simple yet profound. "You see, Herr Gödel, before my time, Europe clung to Roman numerals—cumbersome, rigid, unsuitable for the fluidity of calculation. But during my travels through North Africa and the East, I encountered a different way: the Hindu-Arabic numerals, the system of place value, the beauty of zero." He wiped the dust away and smiled. "I knew then that numbers were meant to be free, flow, and build upon themselves, just as my sequence does. When I returned, I wrote *Liber Abaci*, a book not only about arithmetic but about a new way of seeing numbers—about transformation."

Gödel's eyes flickered with recognition. "Yes, *Liber Abaci*—your great work! It was more than just a book on calculations, wasn't it? It was a revolution. With it, you introduced a system that made mathematics infinitely more powerful. Before you, merchants struggled with clumsy symbols, computations were slow, and yet after your book, commerce, science, and knowledge itself accelerated." He looked toward the spirals in the fountain, the rippling echoes of Fibonacci's numbers. "And yet, Maestro, do you see? The very structure you helped build, this system of numbers we now take for granted, still contains mysteries even you could not have foreseen. It allows us to calculate endlessly, yet within it, there remain truths we can never fully prove."

Fibonacci nodded, eyes gleaming with understanding. "Then we are both witnesses to something greater than ourselves. I revealed a way to see numbers more clearly, and you . . . you have found their limits. And yet, does the fact that some truths lie beyond our reach make them any less beautiful?"

Gödel exhaled, the weight of incompleteness settling upon him once more. "No," he admitted with a quiet smile. "If anything, it makes them more beautiful. Perhaps you are right. The unknown is not a flaw in mathematics—it is its very essence. But tell me, Maestro, when you first saw these numbers unfold before you, did you ever feel as though you were glimpsing something divine? Something beyond human understanding?"

Fibonacci looked up toward the rolling Tuscan sky. "When I saw the pattern emerge when I traced its shape in the petals of flowers and the proportions of great works of art, I knew that I was looking at something eternal. We mathematicians are merely scribes, copying the notes of a great symphony written long before us."

Gödel felt the words settle into him like a deep truth. "Yes," he murmured. "Like Bach's fugues"—*I wish you would meet him,* he thought to himself—"spiraling upon themselves, endlessly recursive, yet never resolving completely." (Gödel knew he was dreaming but did not want to wake up.) "Your sequence is not merely a trick of numbers. It is a bridge between the finite and the infinite."

In the dream, Fibonacci leaned back against the olive tree, a thoughtful expression crossing his face. "It is curious, Herr Gödel, how numbers, once revealed, take on a life of their own."

"Two centuries after you, Maestro, another Leonardo—Leonardo da Vinci—will study the very proportions you uncovered, applying the golden ratio to his paintings, his sketches of the human form, even his architectural designs. He saw what you saw: that nature favors balance, harmony, a divine proportion that governs the petals of flowers, the spirals of shells, and even the symmetry of the human body."

Gödel's fingers moved as if tracing invisible lines in the air. "In his *Vitruvian Man*, in the very composition of Da Vinci's *The Last Supper*, the golden ratio is at work, guiding the placement of figures, the proportions of limbs, the unseen structure beneath beauty."

"Da Vinci turned mathematics into art, just as you turned numbers into a key for understanding nature. He studied proportions as you did, seeing the same underlying order. It is as if your numbers whispered across the centuries, shaping not only equations but masterpieces. And yet, isn't it fascinating? The golden ratio appears so often in nature, in art, and in design, yet no one fully understands why. It is as if the universe prefers this pattern without explanation."

Fibonacci smiled knowingly. "Perhaps some patterns simply are, Herr Gödel. They do not need proof. They exist because they are beautiful, and beauty, like truth, does not always require explanation. They are as if . . . what can I say . . . the expressions of the attributes of a Grand Designer."

Fibonacci chuckled. "Then let us walk upon that bridge together." He gestured toward the courtyard fountain, where water spilled over its edges in near-perfect symmetry. "See there, the spirals in the ripples? Do they not remind you of something? Each new circle born from the sum of the ones before?"

Gödel watched, mesmerized. "Yes. Your sequence, right there in the water."

Fibonacci's eyes twinkled. "Then perhaps, Herr Gödel, the numbers are trying to speak. The question is—are we listening?"

The world around Gödel shimmered. The courtyard, the fountain, and Fibonacci himself—all blurred into a golden spiral, expanding outward in infinite arcs. He felt himself drawn into it, swept along as if following an endless sequence of numbers folding upon themselves.

And then, with a sudden gasp, he awoke.

He was back in his study; the candle burned low, and his notebooks were scattered around him. For a long moment, he simply sat, listening to the silence. Had it been a dream? Or had Fibonacci's numbers truly led him somewhere beyond time?

Gödel turned to his desk, flipping open a blank page. He wrote a single sequence:

1, 1, 2, 3, 5, 8, 13, 21, 34 . . .

He tapped his pen against the table, thinking of spirals, incompleteness, and the beautiful paradox of knowledge. Then, with a knowing smile, he continued writing.

For the sequence never ended. And neither did the search.

CHAPTER FIVE

FRACTALS AND THE FACE OF CHAOS

—Mandelbrot

Clouds are not spheres, mountains are not cones,
coastlines are not circles, and bark is not smooth,
nor does lightning travel in a straight line.

—BENOÎT MANDELBROT (highlighting how natural forms, though seemingly chaotic, possess an underlying mathematical order)

KURT GÖDEL FOUND HIMSELF seated at a small wooden table in the dimly lit warmth of Peter Pratt's Inn, an old colonial tavern nestled in the woods of Yorktown Heights, New York. The air smelled of burning wood and aged oak, and the low hum of conversation flickered like candlelight in the background. He had no recollection of how he had arrived—only that something about the place felt timeless, as though its very walls had absorbed the echoes of centuries.

Across from him, a man with a wild halo of curly hair and sharp, inquisitive eyes stirred his drink absentmindedly. His gaze flickered toward Gödel; a knowing smirk crossing his lips. "You're wondering where you are, aren't you?" The man seemed to be extremely self-aware, able to understand patterns, even the facial patterns of confused travelers.

Gödel straightened, studying the man more closely. "I am beginning to suspect that time and space do not function as expected here."

The man chuckled. "A fair suspicion. In that case, allow me to introduce myself. Benoît Mandelbrot. I suppose you might call me a cartographer of complexity." He tapped the wooden surface of the table with his fingertips. "I study roughness—patterns that seem chaotic at first but reveal an underlying order when viewed the right way."

Mandelbrot had been born in Poland, emigrated to France to escape the Nazis, and eventually moved to the United States in 1958 to work with IBM, where he spent approximately thirty-five years exploring roughness and self-similarity—patterns.

Gödel's brow lifted in recognition. "Yes . . . fractals. Your work has shown that nature repeats itself at every scale, that within what appears disordered, there is an inescapable self-similarity. Clouds, coastlines, mountain ranges—each an infinite recursion of itself."

Mandelbrot nodded. "Precisely. And yet, I suspect you understand better than most that mathematics, for all its elegance, has its limits." He took a sip of his drink, his gaze narrowing. "You showed us that no formal system can be truly complete. That some truths—though real—will forever remain unprovable."

Gödel leaned forward, intrigued. "And you, Professor Mandelbrot, have shown us that some infinities are more structured than we ever imagined. Your fractals—patterns that repeat within themselves at every scale—are echoes of something deeper, as if nature itself is built upon an unending mathematical recursion. Your Mandelbrot set, its edges forever revealing more detail, reminds me of my discoveries. There are truths at the boundary of knowledge that we will never fully capture."

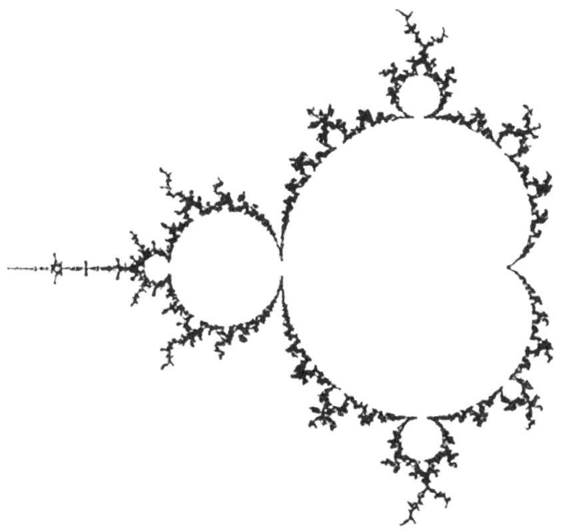

Figure 5. Boundary Mandelbrot, emphasizing the self-similar edge that recurs at every scale. Source: Wikimedia Commons (public domain).

Mandelbrot grinned. "And yet, we still try. That is the beauty of it." He gestured around the old inn. "Think of this place. Over the centuries, it has been rebuilt, expanded, and restored. Yet in each form, it retains its essence. In a way, it follows a fractal pattern—each renovation resembling the structure before it, echoing its past."

Gödel considered this, glancing at the wooden beams above. "Yes. Recursion at work, even in human creations. And, of course, in nature—your fractals reveal that trees, rivers, even the bronchi in our lungs follow a self-similar pattern." He paused, his mind weaving connections. "Strange, isn't it? Fibonacci's sequence appears in nature's proportions, and your fractals reveal nature's infinite complexity. It seems as if we are uncovering the same fundamental order from different directions."

Mandelbrot's eyes gleamed. "Fibonacci, yes! His numbers are everywhere, from the spirals of galaxies to the arrangement of leaves on a stem. And the golden ratio—it crops up in places even I wouldn't have expected." He leaned in, lowering his voice as if sharing a secret. "Did you know that the Mandelbrot set—this chaotic, infinitely detailed object—contains traces of Fibonacci's sequence within it? The ratio of certain iterations approaches the golden ratio as if the two worlds—order and complexity—were never truly separate."

Gödel felt a thrill at the thought. "Then perhaps Fibonacci saw only the beginning. His simple sequence—1, 1, 2, 3, 5, 8—was merely a shadow of something much larger. A glimpse into the infinite."

Mandelbrot's fingers traced a shape on the table—an ever-expanding spiral. "And yet, infinity is never uniform. The coastline of Britain, for instance—if you measure it with a long ruler, you get one answer. If you measure it with a shorter ruler, you get another. The more detail you include, the longer it becomes. It never truly resolves to a single value."

Gödel nodded slowly. "Like knowledge itself. No matter how finely we measure, there will always be more to see, more to prove . . . and more that we never can."

Mandelbrot exhaled, setting his glass down. "So, tell me, Herr Gödel. Does that frustrate you? The idea that some truths—whether in mathematics or nature—will always remain out of reach?"

Gödel considered this carefully. "No," he said at last. "It fascinates me. Infinity is not something to be solved; it is something to be explored. Your fractals, Fibonacci's numbers, my theorems . . . they are all signposts on the same endless journey."

Mandelbrot grinned. "Then perhaps we are explorers of the same landscape, seeing its contours from different angles." A moment of silence passed between them, the weight of understanding settling over the table. Gödel felt as though he had glimpsed something profound—a structure beneath reality itself, vast and unknowable yet endlessly intricate.

Mandelbrot stood, stretching. "Well, Herr Gödel, this has been a most enjoyable encounter. But I suspect the inn will not hold us much longer."

Gödel glanced around, noticing for the first time that the edges of the room seemed to blur as if dissolving into spirals and self-similar shapes. He chuckled softly. "No, I suppose not. Time is . . . flexible in places like this."

Mandelbrot smirked. "Just another fractal unfolding." And with that, the inn, the candlelight, the wooden beams—all dissolved into a swirl of spirals, an infinite regression of shapes folding into themselves. Gödel felt himself drawn into the pattern, into the endless repetition of knowledge and mystery.

When he opened his eyes, he was back in his study. A book on fractals lay open before him, a Fibonacci sequence scrawled in the margins. He exhaled slowly, still feeling the warmth of the old inn, the echo of Mandelbrot's laughter.

And as he reached for his pen, he knew the conversation had only just begun.

CHAPTER SIX

IRREDUCIBLE COMPLEXITY

—C. D. Broad

Induction is the glory of science and the scandal of philosophy.

—C. D. BROAD's paradox (implying that induction is a powerful tool to learn and discover, yet it is embarrassing as we don't understand why it works, unless you accept transcendence)

IT WAS A STRANGE DREAM. Or perhaps something stranger than a dream.

The hallway was long, arched like a cathedral nave, dimly lit by flickering sconces that cast an amber glow on polished stone. Somewhere in the distance, a grandfather clock ticked with an almost sarcastic patience. Time here, it seemed, obeyed different rules—perhaps none at all.

Kurt Gödel walked slowly, his steps making no sound. His mind, as always, was busy with loops. Circles of logic, spirals of self-reference. But this place was not born of logic. It had the scent of metaphysics.

He turned a corner, and there, in a tufted leather chair beside a fireplace that burned without smoke, sat a man reading a book whose title changed each time Gödel tried to read it. The man looked up.

"Ah," he said, his tone crisp and vaguely amused. "Dr. Gödel. I've been expecting you."

The man was tall, lean, with a forehead like a stone archway and eyes that carried the weight of a hundred philosophical lectures.

"C. D. Broad," Gödel said, recognizing him immediately. "The last English metaphysician."

Broad chuckled. "The obituary was premature, I assure you."

Broad (1887–1971) was a Cambridge professor and a prolific thinker of mind, time, perception, ethics, and metaphysics. He was best known for his work *The Mind and Its Place in Nature*, published in 1925 when philosophers still openly wrestled with big metaphysical questions about reality, time, and the mind. But then came the analytical revolution, which grew suspicious of it. Broad was one of the last philosophers before it became intellectually unfashionable to incorporate metaphysics into serious work.

While contemporaries like Bertrand Russell (1872–1970) and Ludwig Wittgenstein (1889–1951) moved philosophy toward linguistic analysis and logical positivism, Broad engaged deeply with questions about consciousness, causation, and the nature of reality. Broad became famous for his articulation of a view called *emergentism*: the view that mental properties arise from complex physical systems (like brains) but are not reducible to the properties of those systems' parts. Broad suggested consciousness is an *emergent property*. His views continue to influence debates on the mind-body problem and the metaphysics of consciousness.

They shook hands. Gödel took the seat across from him. The fire crackled softly, and for a while they simply sat, two minds meeting across the liminal threshold of something not quite time and not quite space.

Broad poured two drinks from a decanter that had not been there a moment ago.

Offering one to Gödel, he said, "What brings the logician to the haunted halls of metaphysics?"

Gödel smiled faintly. "Consciousness, of course. The old ghost that still refuses to be explained away."

Broad leaned back. "Ah, yes. The hard problem that refuses to be flattened by clever chemistry."

"You once proposed," Gödel said, "that some phenomena could be explained only through emergence."

"Strong emergence," Broad corrected. "When irreducible properties and laws appear at higher levels of complexity. Not just epiphenomena—but true novelties. Consciousness, for example."

Gödel nodded. "And yet you argued it was still natural. That these emergent properties, while novel, arose inevitably from the underlying physical substrate."

Broad raised his glass. "Yes. Given the right configuration of matter, new rules emerge. Like steam from water or thought from neurons."

Gödel raised an eyebrow. "But steam does not wonder about itself. Consciousness does."

Broad tilted his head. "Touché."

Gödel leaned in. "Have you heard of Michael Behe?" In 1996, he published *Darwin's Black Box*, which states that complexity discovered by microbiologists has increased significantly over the years, with complexity becoming a deadly challenge to Darwinism.

Broad looked mildly surprised. "A biochemist? He came long after me, then."

Figure 6. The philosopher C. D. Broad (1959). Source: Wikimedia Commons (public domain).

"Yes. But his ideas reach backward."

"Irreducible complexity, yes?" Broad quipped.

Gödel nodded. "Systems composed of interdependent parts that cease to function if even one part is removed. They cannot evolve step by step because intermediate stages are useless. Behe uses it to critique Darwin. Darwin specifically cited complex structures such as the eye as potential stumbling blocks. He openly stated that if it could be demonstrated that any complex organ existed that could not possibly have been formed by numerous successive, slight modifications, his theory would 'absolutely break down.' This statement is found in *On the Origin of Species.*"

In a letter to Asa Gray, the most prominent botanist of the nineteenth century, Darwin repeatedly acknowledged that the lack of intermediate forms was a serious objection, but he argued that further research and a more comprehensive fossil record might resolve this issue. It never did. Not even close.

"I think Behe has something to say about your emergence."

Broad narrowed his eyes. "Explain."

Gödel stood and walked slowly to the fire. "If consciousness is like an irreducibly complex system, then it cannot arise incrementally. There are no partial minds that 'almost work.' *No half qualia.* Either the mind is there, or it is not."

"But my definition of strong emergence allows for such leaps," Broad countered. "Irreducible properties can appear when complexity crosses a certain threshold. The whole becomes more than the sum of the parts."

Gödel turned. "But your threshold assumes something magical happens within the system. That the parts reach a critical mass and the ghost appears. Yet you offer no proof that such thresholds exist—nor that the emergent laws are logically necessitated. You *assume* them."

Broad set his glass down. "So, you claim emergence hides its assumptions."

"Precisely!" Gödel said. "Emergence may simply be a name for what we cannot explain."

Broad looked thoughtful. "Then what would you offer instead?"

Gödel walked to a small writing desk and, with a piece of chalk that had appeared from nowhere, wrote three words on the slate:

Outside the system.

"Like my theorems," he said. "Every consistent formal system has truths it cannot prove from within. Consciousness is such a truth. It knows the system from the outside. It is not generated by the brain—it inhabits it."

Broad stared at the words. The firelight flickered in his eyes.

"You're saying consciousness is not emergent."

"I'm saying it's transcendent. Not supernatural—simply not

derivable. Like the truth of the system's own consistency, which the system itself can never demonstrate."

Broad frowned slightly. "But if we accept that, we must let go of a great deal. We lose the comforting promise that science can, eventually, explain everything."

Gödel's gaze sharpened. "Only if we idolize closure. But science need not be imprisoned by materialism. The real boundary is not what we know but what we allow ourselves to assume."

Broad looked puzzled. "Assume?"

"Yes," Gödel said, pacing now. "The axioms. Every system begins with them. Including science. And if those axioms deny, from the outset, the possibility of something outside—some external source of order, meaning, or mind—then the system is closed like a prison."

He turned. "And what if, in that prison, there is a door leading out—but the prisoner has been trained not to open it?"

Broad stared.

Gödel continued, "Behe shows us that some biological systems cannot be built from the inside out. I show that some logical truths cannot be known from within. And together, these hint at a larger picture: that life and mind are not merely features of matter—they are signals from something beyond."

Broad's voice was quiet now. "But then the scientific method—how can it proceed?"

Gödel smiled gently. "It proceeds better, not worse, when it recognizes its limits. If you believe the whole truth is inside the system, then every contradiction becomes a crisis. But if you allow that some truths come from beyond—then those contradictions become invitations."

"To transcendence," Broad added.

"To humility," Gödel corrected. "And discovery."

Broad sat back. The fire crackled. He looked older now, as though the weight of assumptions had settled visibly on his shoulders.

"I've spent decades tracing the contours of the mind," he said, "thinking that emergence might finally build a bridge from body to soul."

"Perhaps," Gödel said softly, "you were drawing a staircase to a ceiling that does not open. Or perhaps you were standing in a locked room, describing the shadow beneath the door."

They sat in silence.

Broad stood at last. "You may have ruined my theory."

Gödel smiled. "Or elevated it."

They both laughed.

Outside the window, the hallway began to dissolve. The dream was ending.

Broad extended his hand. "You are a troubling guest, Dr. Gödel. But a necessary one."

"And you," Gödel replied, "are a brave host. To invite logic into metaphysics."

They shook hands. And as the dream faded, Broad glanced once more at the chalkboard.

Outside the system.

The words lingered.

Some truths refuse to stay locked inside.

SECTION II

MUSIC AND ART

CHAPTER SEVEN

THE FUGUE OF INFINITY

—Bach

Music is an agreeable harmony for the honor of God and the permissible delights of the soul.

—attributed to JOHANN SEBASTIAN BACH

IT HAD ALL STARTED on a particularly restless night, with Kurt Gödel pacing his study, absorbed in Johann Sebastian Bach's *Musical Offering* patterns. As he listened to Bach's heavenly music, he tranced. The intertwining themes seemed to echo his own mathematical proofs, as though Bach had glimpsed the nature of infinity in music centuries before Gödel had formalized it in numbers. "If only I could ask him . . . how did he see the patterns?" he murmured aloud, feeling the weight of his own incompleteness theorems, those strange results that proved that some truths would always remain beyond logic's grasp.

And then, inexplicably, the room around him shifted. A strange, rippling sensation took over as though he were falling through the spaces between Bach's notes. Suddenly, he found himself standing in a grand, candlelit church, surrounded by the delicate, interwoven sound of a fugue. Somehow, he had been transported to Leipzig in 1747, to the very place and time where Johann Sebastian Bach was at the organ, playing in the quiet sanctuary of Saint Thomas Church. He was not sure he was awake, was full of self-doubt, and did not want to interrupt whatever he was feeling.

With disbelief and awe, Gödel gathered his thoughts and, after a time of reflection, approached the composer. He knew it was Bach, as he was playing the cantata known as *God Is My King* (BWV 71). "Maestro Bach," he called softly, trying to contain his excitement, "your music is . . . astounding. The way each theme folds back into itself as if it could go on forever . . . it reminds me of a proof, of a logical structure."

Bach turned, studying the stranger with a calm but curious gaze, his hands still resting lightly on the keys. Bach was not famous during his lifetime (1685–1750). He was primarily known as an organist, and his music was only appreciated by a few connoisseurs. It was nearly eighty years after his death that Bach was rediscovered when Felix Mendelssohn conducted a performance of Bach's *Saint Matthew Passion* in Berlin and when his first biography was published. He immediately became one of the greatest composers of all time. His music became synonymous with baroque music.

As Bach was interrupted by Gödel, he quipped, "Ah, so you hear the patterns," as if testing the honesty of Gödel. Bach continued, "Few listeners do, but I am pleased you hear it. You speak of logical structures; are you a man of mathematics?"

Gödel's eyes brightened. "Yes! I study mathematical proofs, structures that build upon themselves like the themes in your fugues. Each step connects to the last, forming something whole and complete." But he hesitated. "I have discovered something unusual. There are beautiful and inevitable truths that cannot be proven within any logical system. They remain out of reach as if beyond the very structure they're part of."

Bach hovered his fingers over the keys, frozen in thought. "Truths that cannot be proven . . . it sounds much like faith, something known but not fully understood. Tell me, Herr . . . ?"

"Gödel. Kurt Gödel," he said quickly, bowing slightly, realizing how surreal this introduction felt. "Your music inspired my journey here, Maestro. I wondered if you might reveal how you see these patterns so clearly. The counterpoint, the canon—your compositions seem to echo something eternal, almost as if they were recursive, looping endlessly."

Bach chuckled, pressing a soft chord that resonated through the empty church. "Then let me play you something, Herr Gödel, that may explain it better than words. Listen here: This is a canon. The melody responds to itself, each voice entering, replying, and returning." He began to play, the melody wrapping around itself, each voice imitating and mirroring the other in perfect harmony. "Do you hear it? The music feels like it could continue forever, yet we only hear a fragment of what might be."

Gödel listened in amazement. "Yes! It's as if it's hinting at something infinite, a pattern that never truly ends, only cycling back into itself, like a spiral that goes on and on. Maestro, this is precisely like *recursion*—a function or a proof that repeats itself endlessly, self-contained yet always evolving. I see something similar in my mathematics. Imagine an equation that references itself—no matter how far you follow it, you'll never truly reach the end."

Bach nodded thoughtfully, his fingers still moving across the keys. "Then perhaps, Herr Gödel, both your mathematics and my music reach toward something we cannot fully grasp. A mystery that continues within itself, always unfolding." He paused, looking intently at Gödel. "Yet you say these truths of yours cannot be proven. What does that mean?"

"It means that no matter how advanced our logical systems become, there will always be truths that lie outside of what we can formally prove. They exist, they influence, yet they are forever just beyond reach." Gödel's voice softened, almost reverent. "It is like your fugues, Maestro. They feel whole and complete, yet each phrase opens into something new, as though no single moment could contain the entire truth."

Figure 7. An excerpt from Johann Sebastian Bach's *Toccata and Fugue in D Minor* (BWV 565). Source: Bach-Gesellschaft Ausgabe, 1867 (public domain).

Bach leaned back slightly, considering this. "That is a strange idea—completeness with something missing. Perhaps you are right; in music, as in life, we glimpse what we cannot fully hold. Tell me, is this why you have journeyed here, from . . . wherever you've come from?"

Gödel hesitated, marveling again at the sheer improbability of this conversation. "Yes. I had to know how you saw these patterns so clearly, how you composed something as complex as a fugue or a canon with such precision. Did you intend it to feel infinite, recursive?"

Bach's eyes gleamed. "Not at first, no. But then I found that the more I wove themes together, the more they seemed to suggest infinity on their own, each note pointing to the next and the next as if echoing something greater. It is as though the music itself leads me, Herr Gödel. In composing, I am only following."

Gödel felt a shiver at this. "Following . . . yes, I feel that as well. As though each discovery is only a step on an endless path, leading to something beyond even logic. Yet in mathematics, there's an urge to reach completion, to prove everything, as if finding a perfect chord." He looked at Bach intently. "But I've shown that perfection may never come. Like your canon, some ideas are endless—they open door after door without ever fully resolving."

Bach nodded with a quiet smile. "Much like faith, Herr Gödel. We live with this tension: to believe, to create, and yet to accept that some mysteries remain. Music, too, echoes the infinite, reminding us that in every note, there is something just beyond reach."

Bach's fingers danced over the keys again, filling the room with sound. "Here, this fugue—listen. Each theme chases the other, resolving only when I, the player, *choose* to end it."

Gödel closed his eyes, letting the music unfold around him like a tapestry made of thought. Each melody line echoed the others, folding back, rising, repeating—not randomly, but with a purpose just shy of being revealed.

"It's beautiful," he whispered. "And . . . incomplete."

Bach looked over, one eyebrow raised.

"I mean that as a compliment," Gödel added quickly. "Your fugue could continue. I feel it. It wants to. It hints at something beyond the final note—as if it exists outside time, waiting to be played again, in another key, on another day."

Bach laughed softly, his hands now resting in his lap. "Perhaps that's the point, Herr Gödel. Maybe a fugue is never truly finished—only paused. Left hovering like a question with no last word."

Gödel was quiet for a moment, the echo of the final chord still vibrating through the wood of the pews. "That's it, isn't it? You've composed something that reflects the shape of truth itself—curved, recursive, unfinished. My theorems tell me there are things we can never fully prove. But your music shows me . . . that maybe that's not a failure."

Bach smiled, rising slowly from the bench. "And your mathematics tells me that what we cannot prove might still be true."

They stood in silence beneath the great vaulted ceiling. The flickering candlelight made shadows of the organ pipes, tall and silent now, like a forest of thought.

"Maestro," Gödel said, "do you believe there is a final resolution? A place where the fugue ends—not because someone stops playing, but because the music finds its home?"

Bach walked to the center of the sanctuary and turned, his face thoughtful. "I believe," he said, "that every theme, every counterpoint, every dissonance . . . longs for harmony. Even if we never hear the final chord, it exists. Not in the air, perhaps—but in the mind of the Composer."

Gödel's breath caught. He stared at Bach—not the historical figure now, not the genius—but the man. A man who had lived his life listening for something beyond the reach of notes.

"A Composer?" Gödel asked quietly.

Bach nodded. "Of course. You see patterns in numbers. I hear them in sound. But the patterns themselves . . . they come from somewhere."

Gödel smiled softly. "Or *someone*."

Bach stepped forward and extended his hand. "Perhaps we are each writing footnotes in the margins of a greater score."

Gödel took his hand, the moment strangely solemn. "Yes. And your music gave me the courage to accept what logic could not finish."

The candles flickered as if in agreement. Outside, a bell began to toll—deep, slow, echoing through the darkened streets of Leipzig.

Bach turned toward the organ once more. "Shall I play one last piece for you, Herr Gödel?"

"Please."

He sat and began again—not with a fugue this time, but a simple chorale. The melody was plain, almost humble. But it glowed. And as the harmonies rose, Gödel felt something loosen in him—not an answer, but peace with not knowing.

The final chord rang out and faded into silence.

Then the light shifted.

The church faded.

And Gödel was once again in his study, alone with his thoughts and the stillness of the night.

But something had changed.

The silence now felt musical.

As if somewhere, just beyond hearing, the fugue continued.

CHAPTER EIGHT

HANDS THAT DRAW THEMSELVES

—M. C. Escher

I don't belong anywhere anymore . . . I hover between mathematics and art.

—M. C. ESCHER

THERE IS A MOMENT when a painter lifts his brush and touches the canvas, and for a brief instant, the world changes. Out of blankness, a mark. Out of silence, a whisper. In that fragile gesture lies a mystery as old as thought itself: **Can something finite ever capture the infinite?**

Art is the miracle of containment without confinement, of building windows into the eternal with the frail timber of human hands. We reach for the ineffable through our crafts, whether on the taut surface of a canvas, the vibrating string of a cello, or the fragile lattice of mathematical symbols. Somewhere deep within us, there is an instinct—perhaps divine, perhaps desperate—that insists that what is infinite must leave a trace.

The mathematician feels it, too, when symbols swirl on a page and an idea leaps beyond itself. The musician feels it when a sequence of notes seems to spiral into a place beyond hearing. Each creator, in his own tongue, chases the same elusive quarry: to capture the shadow of infinity in mortal form.

It was in such a mood that Kurt Gödel found himself once again drifting, half in thought, half in dream. His mind, ever restlessly reaching, had been pondering a lithograph that had seized his imagination like few things outside of pure logic could.

M. C. ESCHER'S *DRAWING HANDS*

Two hands, each drawing the other into existence.

A paradox made visible. A loop from which there is no exit, only deeper wonder.

He had stared at it for hours earlier that afternoon, unable to pull away, marveling at the simplicity of the idea and the enormity of its implications. Here, in black and white, was a truth he had spent a lifetime trying to whisper into the ears of mathematicians: There is no absolute foundation unless there is an external perspective (the viewer in this case). There is only the mutual support of structures that define themselves in a kind of dance.

If only, Gödel mused, he could step inside that drawing. If only he could speak to the mind that had conceived it.

As if the thought had bent reality, the world around him softened. The study where he sat melted into the outlines of a different place—a room with tall windows, where the late afternoon light broke into soft pools on worn wooden floors. The smell of ink and old paper was rich and alive, and the faint sound of scratching pencils echoed like music.

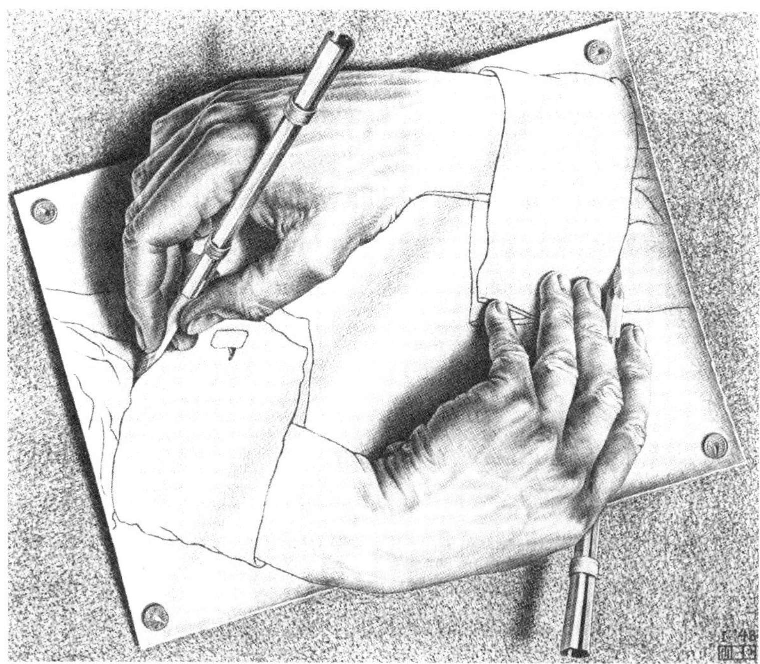

Figure 8. Source: M. C. Escher's *Drawing Hands* www.mcescher.com.

Maurits Cornelis Escher, though not trained as a mathematician, had become a master of visual logic. A Dutch graphic artist with an eye for impossible architecture and recursive geometry, he created worlds that bent gravity, defied dimension, and danced on the edge of paradox.

Escher—born in 1898 in the Frisian town of Leeuwarden, the Netherlands—had wandered far from his northern roots. Trained briefly in architecture, he found his true compass while sketching the Moorish tessellations of the Alhambra in Granada, Spain, and the Romanesque cloisters of southern Italy. Where most painters chased impressions, Escher chased symmetries: tiling that locked together like crystalline prayers, staircases that climbed into themselves, and waterfalls that poured forever uphill.

Without the scaffolding of formal mathematics, he taught himself the language of infinity with nothing but a compass, a straightedge, and relentless curiosity. It was his devotion to disciplined imagination—the very quality of seeking the infinite within well-ruled bounds—that made him a kindred spirit to any logician searching for the edges of reason.

Works like *Relativity*, with its staircases looping in conflicting directions, and *Ascending and Descending*, where figures climb endlessly but go nowhere, revealed his fascination with the limits of perception and the illusions that structure our understanding of reality. His drawings were not just images but invitations—portals into thought experiments where the laws of logic and space are both followed and broken.

Before Gödel, bent intently over a large drafting table, was a man, lean and deliberate, dressed simply but meticulously. His hands, long and precise, moved like a magician's, conjuring impossible forms from the emptiness.

Maurits Cornelis Escher looked up with a warm but curious expression, as if he had been expecting Gödel all along.

"Ah," Escher said in Dutch-tinged English, setting down his pencil. "You are the one who draws with symbols."

Gödel smiled. "And you," he said, stepping closer, "are the one who draws with impossibility."

They laughed—a dry, mutual laugh, knowing and admiring. Without the need for explanation, the conversation between them unfurled like a ribbon tossed into the air.

"Tell me," Gödel began, his voice soft with wonder, "when you made *Drawing Hands*, what were you chasing?"

Escher leaned back, contemplating. His eyes, sharp and playful, gleamed under thick brows. "A game, at first. A simple game. I was fascinated by loops, by structures that fold back onto themselves. But as I worked, it grew. It became . . ."—he searched for the word—"a meditation. On dependence. On creation."

Gödel nodded, feeling the resonance deep in his chest.

"Self-reference," he said. "Circularity. The foundation and the fracture of knowledge itself."

Escher's mouth twitched in a half smile. "In art, as in life, there is no clean beginning. Each line calls forth the next. Each hand, drawing the other, must trust that it is not alone."

Gödel turned to look again at the lithograph now hanging behind Escher on the wall. The hands—poised mid-creation, caught forever in the act of bringing each other into being—seemed to pulse with life.

"In mathematics," Gödel said slowly, "I showed that any system rich enough to speak of numbers will harbor truths it cannot prove. There are statements that exist within the system that can only be seen from beyond it."

Escher's brow furrowed slightly in thought. "And yet the system lives, incomplete."

"Exactly," Gödel said. "Just as your hands live, forever unfinished, forever becoming."

Escher leaned forward. "But in art, there is a different mercy. The incompleteness is part of the beauty. In mathematics, perhaps, it is a wound."

Gödel smiled, a sad, knowing smile. "Not a wound, my friend. A window."

They paused, both men standing in the heavy, beautiful silence that only profound recognition brings.

Escher reached into a drawer and pulled out several sketches, then spread them across the table. Impossible staircases, hands reaching into and out of frames, fish morphing into birds and back again.

"I have tried," he said quietly, "to draw the infinite in forms the eye can see. But it always escapes."

Escher reached toward one of the prints and turned it slightly toward Gödel.

"This one is called *Relativity*. I imagined a world where gravity points in multiple directions, depending on your frame of reference. People walk sideways, climb upside down, and yet—within each path, everything still makes sense."

Gödel studied the impossible staircases, the figures gliding in solemn routines on planes that should never coexist.

"Fascinating," he murmured. "Each group obeys its own laws . . . yet the whole cannot be unified without contradiction."

Escher nodded. "And yet, the illusion feels complete. You almost believe it—until you try to step into it yourself."

Gödel's voice lowered. "It is the same in mathematics. Within a formal system, everything may seem perfectly sound . . . until you realize that no single perspective can encompass all truths unless you step outside the system. You ascend and descend yet remain on the same level."

Gödel tapped the image gently.

"In *Relativity*, as in logic, perspective defines what seems real, but not all could be true. But if you try to accept and reconcile all perspectives at once—you break the frame."

"It must," Gödel said. "For if you could capture it fully, it would cease to be infinite."

Escher nodded, tracing the edge of one drawing with a fingertip. "Then the point is not to catch it but to chase it."

"Yes," Gödel whispered. "To point toward it. To create signposts for souls hungry for what lies beyond the visible."

The late sunlight deepened, turning the room into a cathedral of shadows and gold.

"When I listen to Bach," Gödel said, his voice hushed, "I hear patterns unfolding, folding back on themselves, hinting at something larger. In your work, I *see* it. Infinity glimpsed in finite strokes."

Escher smiled, a rare softness touching his usually sharp features.

"Then perhaps," he said, "we are all architects of the unseen."

"Yes," Gödel said. "And each drawing, each theorem, each note—a reaching hand."

They stood together, two men from different worlds, united by a longing neither could fully name. Between them, the *Drawing Hands* hovered—an emblem of endless creation, endless hunger, endless beauty.

The silence stretched long and full. The kind of silence that does not demand to be broken.

At last, Gödel spoke, his voice little more than a breath.

"Art," he said, "is the mirror that teaches us how to love what we cannot possess."

Escher's eyes glistened faintly. "And mathematics is the proof that there is more than we can ever hold."

A gentle wind stirred the papers on the table. The room shimmered, and for a fleeting instant, Gödel thought he saw the very edge of reality curl like a sheet of paper lifted by unseen hands.

And then he was alone again, in his study. The evening deepened outside his window.

But in his heart, the hands still moved, drawing and being drawn, forever chasing, forever becoming.

And for that moment, it was enough.

CHAPTER NINE

THE ETERNAL PROPORTIONS

—Vitruvius

The length of a man's outspread arms is equal to his height.

—LEONARDO DA VINCI

IMAGINE A SUNLIT AFTERNOON tinged with the scent of citrus and the distant melody of laughter—a day when you, the curious wanderer, might chance upon a secret meeting between eras. After surreal and mind-tickling conversations with Fibonacci, Mandelbrot, Bach, and Escher, Kurt Gödel found himself bubbling with anticipation while reading and admiring *De Architectura*, a comprehensive guide to Roman classical architecture.

"What hidden wonders might the architectural genius of Vitruvius reveal?" he mused. The air itself seemed charged with possibility, as if the universe were inviting him to step into another chapter of endless discovery.

In one electrifying moment, time whirled like the vibrant strokes of a master painter's brush. One moment, Gödel was lost in thought in his study, and the next, he was standing in an ancient Roman courtyard where every stone told a story and every ripple of a fountain sang a ballad of perfect proportions. It was the world of Vitruvius—a realm where architecture and art merged in a delightful symphony. And you, dear reader, are welcome to join him on this extraordinary escapade.

Gödel's heart pounded with a mix of awe and excitement as he took in his surroundings. The courtyard was alive with color and history: sun-dappled marble walls draped in vibrant ivy and a majestic fountain whose water cascaded in mesmerizing, spiraling patterns. This was not a place confined to dusty history books; it was a living, breathing work of art waiting to share its secrets.

As Gödel strolled along the ancient walkway, his eyes caught a familiar yet timeless figure. Beneath a grand cypress tree that seemed to whisper legends of old, a dignified yet playful man was engrossed in sketching intricate geometric forms on a weathered scroll. This was Vitruvius, the master of proportions, whose ideas would later spark a Renaissance rebirth—a marvel that painted the faces of da Vinci and Michelangelo with newfound brilliance.

Born in the first century BC, Vitruvius was not merely an architect but a visionary polymath whose treatise, *De Architectura*, distilled the essence of Roman engineering and aesthetic perfection. His writings outlined that the beauty of a structure was not only in its strength and durability but also in the harmonious proportions that echoed nature's own design. Vitruvius championed the concept that buildings should mirror the symmetry and balance of the human body, a philosophy that reverberated across millennia. His clear, methodical observations led him to document everything from the proper spacing of columns to the delicate balance needed in water supply systems and fortifications. He provided detailed accounts of how arches, vaults, and even the layout of cities could be optimized for both functionality and beauty.

Vitruvius's genius was evident in projects that still inspire awe today. Consider the design of the modular temple, where every column and cornice adhered to strict proportional guidelines, or the ingenious aqueducts that not only provided life-sustaining water but also enhanced the urban landscape with their elegant, sweeping arches. His practical wisdom extended to military engineering, where he designed fortifications that were both formidable and aesthetically pleasing. The influence of *De Architectura* would ripple through the ages, inspiring the imaginations of Renaissance architects such as Leon Battista Alberti and Andrea Palladio. Both Alberti's and Palladio's writings and buildings helped define Renaissance architectural ideals and had a lasting impact on the European architectural environment and beyond.

They saw in Vitruvius's words a bridge to a lost perfection, one they eagerly recreated in their own designs, shaping the very vision of modern Western architecture. Alberti's *De Pictura* introduced the concept of the linear perspective of a three-dimensional space on a two-dimensional surface. Palladio's villas and palace designs reflected the influence of Vitruvius on Renaissance beauty.

With a twinkle in his eye, Vitruvius looked up and greeted Gödel as if welcoming an old friend from a far-off future. "Well, aren't you a curious spirit? You seem to have stepped out of time itself, my friend. Tell me, do you come from a world where numbers and ideas have taken flight, where the secrets of beauty in art and structure still puzzle the soul?"

Gödel couldn't help but smile at the unmistakable joy in Vitruvius's tone. "Indeed, I do," he replied, his voice full of wonder. "In my time, I've danced with the mysteries of Fibonacci and marveled at the infinite patterns discovered by Mandelbrot. Yet here, amid the grandeur of ancient Rome, I find myself captivated by your art—the way every column sings a note in the symphony of the cosmos, every arch echoes the eternal balance of nature."

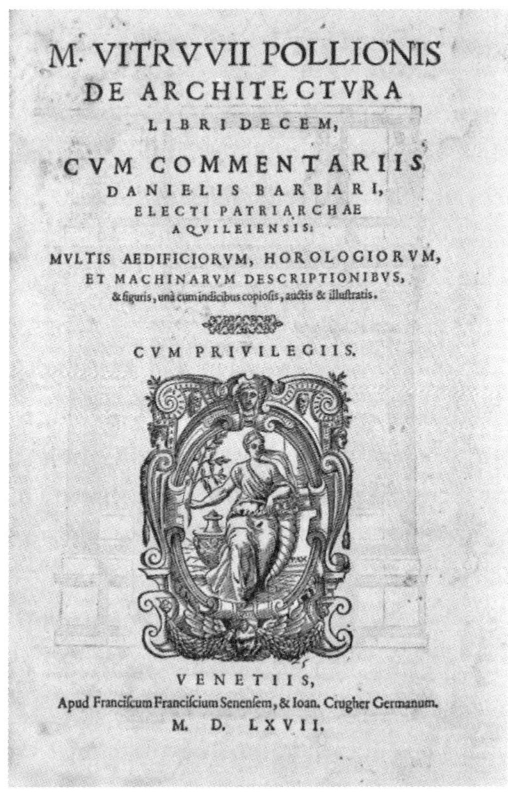

M· VITRVVII POLLIONIS
DE ARCHITECTVRA
LIBRI DECEM,
CVM COMMENTARIIS
DANIELIS BARBARI,
ELECTI PATRIARCHAE
AQVILEIENSIS:
MVLTIS AEDIFICIORVM, HOROLOGIORVM,
ET MACHINARVM DESCRIPTIONIBVS,
& figuris, unà cum indicibus copioſis, auctis & illuſtratis.

CVM PRIVILEGIIS.

VENETIIS,
Apud Franciſcum Franciſcium Senenſem, & Ioan. Crugher Germanum.
M. D. LXVII.

Figure 9. Ornate allegorical vignette featuring Vitruvius surrounded by architectural tools and symbols, marking the start of the *Ten Books*. Source: 1550 edition with commentaries by Daniel Barbarus, *M. Vitruvii Pollionis De Architectura libri decem.*

Gödel asked, "Have you asked yourself why?"

Vitruvius, as if confused, said, "Do you mean why nature and beauty contain proportions that simply appear as part of an orderly design? I have often wondered and assumed it is some divine proportion that has been imputed into the universe."

"Exactly!" responded Gödel.

The conversation deepened as they ambled along the colonnaded path. Vitruvius recalled the meticulous care with which he had designed the Capitoline Temple and other civic structures, ensuring that even as they withstood the tests of time and nature, they also delighted the human spirit with their grace. "I remember ensuring that the spacing of the Doric columns wasn't arbitrary, but calculated to reflect a cosmic harmony," he explained, his voice warm with recollection. "And when constructing aqueducts, I realized they could serve a dual purpose—quenching the thirst of a burgeoning city and creating vistas that lifted the spirit, much like a well-composed piece of music."

Gödel paused, letting the memory of ancient Rome's bustling forums and serene public baths wash over him. "It fills me with delight that centuries after your insights, masters like da Vinci will take your musings on proportion and infuse them into art. The *Vitruvian Man*, for instance, stands as a testament to how deeply intertwined the beauty of the human form is with the structural elegance of buildings."

Vitruvius's eyes gleamed with pride—not of vanity, but of knowing that his work had kindled the flames of creativity in future generations.

Gödel leaned closer, his own passion for abstract truths melding with the tangible legacy before him. "And yet," he murmured, "even as we capture nature's beauty through these divine proportions, there's a secret twist—a playful mystery that forever dances just beyond our grasp. In every system that dares to encapsulate arithmetic, there lingers a truth that simply cannot be proven within its own confines. It's like constructing a magnificent edifice that, no matter how flawless its design, always leaves a door ajar to the infinite."

The words danced in the air like shimmering light on water, inviting you to lean in closer and become part of this enchanting dialogue. Picture it: two brilliant minds—one ancient and wise, the other a modern seeker of truth—engaging in a conversation that transcended time. Their exchange was vibrant, alive with contagious enthusiasm for discovery, and made you want to jump right into the conversation yourself.

Vitruvius chuckled, tracing a graceful curve in the dust with his stylus. "You see, dear friend, my columns and arches are more than mere stone. They are the melody of the cosmos made manifest, *an open invitation to explore, to wonder, and to embrace the sublime beauty of imperfection.* Like a masterful painting, every structure holds within it a hint of mystery—a dash of the infinite that makes it endlessly enchanting."

Gödel nodded and then replied, his voice low and sincere. "Exactly so. In mathematics, as in architecture, the magic resides in the quest itself. To appreciate and ponder art, a structure, a painting, or a sculpture, each must be seen by an *outsider*. Art cannot appreciate and critique itself; it demands a verdict. In the same way, every theorem we prove, every structure we build, only hints at a grander design—a design that, by its very nature, is never fully complete. And isn't that the most wondrous part? It invites us to keep questioning, keep seeking, and keep marveling at what might yet be discovered."

For a few precious moments, they sat in a shared silence, soaking in the beauty of the timeless courtyard—its ancient stones, its dancing fountain, its promise of endless mystery.

For a moment, the garden seemed to hold its breath—marble and marble dust suspended between stone and spirit. Gödel and

Vitruvius rose from the bench, their conversation tapering into a shared smile of recognition: that no matter how perfectly one might craft a column or prove a theorem, something always remains just beyond reach.

Vitruvius rested a hand on the fluted shaft of a column, tracing its curve as one might follow the graceful line of a musical phrase. "Each of my buildings," he murmured, "was meant to evoke the harmony of nature. Yet in every temple and aqueduct, there lies an intentional pause—an interval, if you will—where human craftsmanship meets the infinite."

Gödel nodded, eyes reflecting sunlight and shadows intermingled. "And in every formal system I've studied, their lives an unprovable statement—a silent doorway that beckons the mind outward. Just as your architecture invites the eye to wander past the stone, so too does mathematics invite the heart to glimpse the boundless."

They walked on, footfalls echoing lightly through the colonnade. The fountain's water, caught in a spiral of light, reminded you that even the most rigid geometry yields to fluid motion—just as a proof yields to the subtle dance of the unprovable. There, in the hush between their words, the courtyard revealed its secret: that beauty is never a closed system but an open question.

As twilight began to gild the courtyard, Vitruvius turned to Gödel. "Perhaps the true symmetry," he said softly, "lies not only in the ratios of columns to pediments, but in the way our minds reach beyond them."

Gödel smiled, lifting his gaze to where the first stars of evening peeked through an archway. "Yes," he replied, "for it is the act of seeking—in art or arithmetic—that gives life to the infinite. In our best designs and our deepest proofs, we leave a door unlatched. And through that door, imagination wanders into the sublime."

You, dear reader, stand now at that threshold. Behind you, the sure geometry of stone and theorem; before you, a landscape of possibility. May you step forward with the same courage of mind and spirit, ever ready to discover the whispers that lie beyond the perfect line.

And so, their dialogue closed—not with an answer but with an open question, echoing through marble halls and numbered axioms alike: *What wonders await when we embrace the beautiful incompleteness of all things?*

CHAPTER TEN

SCIVIAS AND NEUMES

—Hildegard von Bingen

Art is a collaboration between God and the artist, and the less the artist does, the better.

—ANDRÉ PAUL GUILLAUME GIDE

KURT GÖDEL SAT LATE in his institute study, this time with pages of bright illustrations spread before him, utterly absorbed by their luminous illuminations—swirling mandalas of ruby and gold—uncanny creatures rendered in fluid, almost modern abstraction and vines that curled into secret alphabets of light. He marveled at how the art seemed to pulse with an inner glow, each leaf and angelic figure born of visions rather than the hand alone.

Gödel was admiring the *Frontispiece of Scivias*, showing Hildegard von Bingen receiving a vision, dictating, and sketching on a wax tablet. What truths lay in those flickering "flames" above her head—words that no eye but hers could fully decipher? Gödel, peering at this scene, saw in Hildegard's inspired script the same paradox he found in arithmetic: visions that pointed beyond every line and letter to a realm no formal system can wholly capture. Beauty that could only come from *above*.

As he traced a circle of sapphire ink, a sudden vertigo seized him—his lamplit walls blurred, the hush of his bookshelves dissolved—and in the next moment he found himself stepping through a carved wooden door into a cloistered courtyard, stone walls warmed by the pale glow of lanterns. The year was 1141—this felt all the stranger to Gödel, accustomed as he was to the precise demarcations of modern time. Hildegard von Bingen stirred in the predawn hush of the Disibodenberg monastery's guest chamber, the faint scent of incense lingering in the cool air. She had risen early, as she often did, to capture the visions that came in the earliest light.

Disibodenberg monastery, built in the seventh century, spread its arms in a grand embrace of stone and sky. When Hildegard first beheld it, it was a vast rectangular cloister lined by soaring arcades of pale limestone—each molded column crowned by carved capitals lush with vine motifs and saintly visages. Behind those walls lay a sunlit courtyard of emerald grass, bisected by narrow flagstone paths that led pilgrims to a central well, its moss-covered lip echoing the steady drip of nearby springs. In every corner, slender lancet windows framed the forest's green hush, and the half-hidden organ chamber resonated with faint drafts of wind through its wooden shutters. Above, the lofty roof—now vanished—must once have sheltered choir and scribes alike, its timbers echoing with the soft scrape of quills and the radiant swell of Hildegard's first chants, as though the very stones themselves yearned to carry her visions into eternity.

Hildegard, who later founded and became abbess of Rupertsberg, was in her early forties when Gödel's strange visit occurred. She seemed to be waiting for him already, her robes whispering on the flagstones.

A DIVINE VISION OF ART

Word of Hildegard von Bingen's gifts had traveled slowly through the cloisters of the Rhine throughout the twelfth century. She was renowned among the small circle of nuns who shared her devotion, but beyond that, even fellow Benedictines knew little of the woman whose eyes seemed to hold luminous truth.

Born in 1098 in Böckelheim (near modern-day Frankfurt), she had been offered as an oblate at the convent of Disibodenberg at the tender age of eight. By 1136, she had been elected magistra (mother superior). There, she claimed she first heard the voice of the divine calling her to describe "the living light."

Over the decades, Hildegard's clairvoyant visions coalesced into writings: *Scivias* ("Know the Ways," an illustrated work of art that described multiple religious visions), *Liber Vitae Meritorum* ("The Book of Rewards of Life," a volume of visionary theology, morality, human flaws, virtues and vices), and *Liber Divinorum Operum* ("The Book of Divine Works," a book of divine visions and illustrations with mandalas that resembled Mandelbrot's fractals). Few dared to read these works, for they brimmed with startling imagery: wheel-like mandalas spinning with angels, rivers of red flame, and creatures half eagle, half man. Later, as the abbess of Rupertsberg, she gathered her closest sisters to transcribe these revelations into her many books of wonder.

Gödel's first glimpse of Hildegard was through a narrow window of the chapel. The high, arched ceiling soared above a simple choir of wooden benches. Flickering candles danced on carved pillars that depicted vine motifs, every leaf rendered with painstaking care—each a work of devotion. In the center, Hildegard knelt before an altar draped in emerald-green cloth, her hands folded around a psalter bound in sheepskin. A small sistrum—an instrument like a rattle of linked metal rings—rested on a nearby shelf, waiting for the next feast day's liturgy. In the corner, a reed organ hummed softly as though in anticipation, its tiny pipes ready to supply the drones and bass notes that underlay Hildegard's soaring melodies.

Figure 10. Portrait of German abbess and physician Hildegard von Bingen. Source: Wikimedia Commons (public domain).

For the first moment, Gödel watched in silence. He recognized a kindred spirit in her intensity: The seriousness with which he devoted himself to questions of logic was now mirrored in her fervent gaze. He stepped forward, making no sound, as though he were part of the wall's pattern.

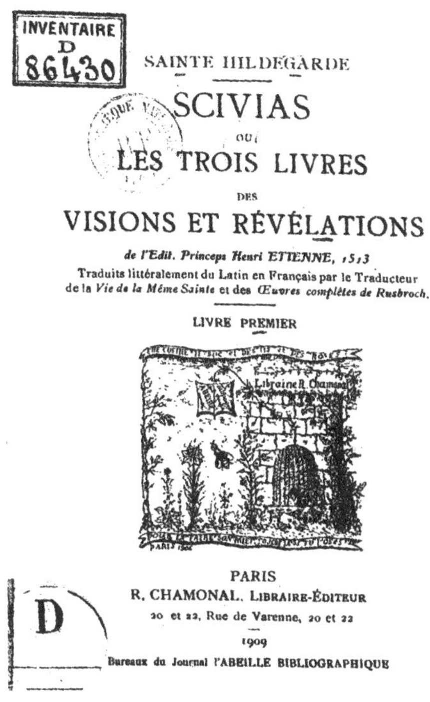

SAINTE HILDEGARDE

SCIVIAS

OU

LES TROIS LIVRES

DES

VISIONS ET RÉVÉLATIONS

de l'Edit. Princeps Henri ETIENNE, 1513

Traduits littéralement du Latin en Français par le Traducteur de la *Vie de la Même Sainte* et des *Œuvres complètes de Rusbroch.*

LIVRE PREMIER

PARIS

R. CHAMONAL, Libraire-Éditeur

20 et 22, Rue de Varenne, 20 et 22

1909

Bureaux du Journal l'ABEILLE BIBLIOGRAPHIQUE

Figure 11. Title page of *Scivias, ou Les trois livres de visions et révélations* by Sainte Hildegarde. Source: Wikimedia Commons (public domain).

Hildegard rose slowly, as if sensing his presence. At first, her eyes widened—part wonder, part calm recognition. To her, Gödel did not appear as a ghost nor as a myth; he was simply another soul drawn by the currents of her frequent revelations. She inclined her head, welcoming him. In that gesture, centuries of solitude and meditation borrowed a new meaning.

THE MUSIC AND THE MYSTERY

"Venerable abbess," Gödel began, choosing his words slowly and carefully, for the Latin of the twelfth century differed from the

German in which he often thought. "My name is Kurt Gödel. I come from a distant future to inquire about your art and the source of your inspirations. Your sisters speak of visions, lights, colors, forms they cannot name. I sense art that reveals truths that lie beyond the surface of symbols. I have sought similar experiences, but grounded in logic and mathematics. I wonder: How do you know that a vision is *true and good?*"

Hildegard guided him to a bench carved from local oak. Through the stained-glass windows, rose-hued dawn light filtered in, painting the cloister floor with petals of colored glass. She placed her hand on the psalter.

"Truth comes," she said softly, "as the air carries incense. One inhales it; one does not fabricate it. When I hear the melody of the living light, I am compelled to sing it for others—lest the world forget the river that flows from the heavenly court. Truth is not something we create; it is something we *receive.* Yet, to record it, I must find a form—notes on parchment, words on vellum—though *those forms can never fully capture* the divine richness."

Gödel nodded. He understood that tension. His incompleteness theorems had shown him that any formal system—arithmetic built from a finite set of axioms—could not prove all truths about itself.

"In my work," he said, "I showed that any system powerful enough to express the simplest statements about numbers could never be both complete and consistent. It must, if it aspires to prove its own integrity, rely on an axiom that comes from outside. In a sense, *every proof requires something extrinsic*—just as I hear the truth of mathematics but cannot prove that truth using only the system's internal rules."

Hildegard's gaze shifted toward the slender host of candles at the nave's far end. Their flames flickered, as though tempting her to ignite her reply.

"Your axioms, Master Gödel," she replied, "are like the first syllables of wings before a melody. I, too, rely on something *beyond* my manuscript. I hum the notes as they come to me—my sisters copy them onto thin strips of handled parchment. But those notes are only shadows of the pure sound I perceive in my ecstasies. I call the book of my music *Symphonia armonie celestium revelationum*—symphony of the harmony of celestial revelations. Yet, those words do not create the melody; *they merely describe what comes from another source*."

THE INSTRUMENTS OF HEAVEN

Leaning back, Gödel considered the reed organ, its circular shape hinting at infinity within finitude. "You mention *Symphonia*," he said. "Why do you choose instruments such as the organ or the psaltery? Do they not constrain the song? Could there be pure revelation without music—just voices alone?"

Hildegard's smile rippled with both mirth and gravity. "Voices are like lines on a page without punctuation. The organs give us breath; they offer chords that resonate in the chest. The psaltery's strings tremble in the hand as if the universe itself quivers at the touch of God. Without an instrument or a chant, a vision remains solitary—proper to the one soul who sees. But when I sing and play alongside it, the vision becomes communal. It enters the hearts of the others."

She rose and moved to the organ. With practiced fingers, she pressed a key, and a low drone emerged—a hum so gentle that, at first, it appeared to be the beating of her own heart. Then, lifting her eyes to an imaginary point high in the chapel's vault, she launched into a melody from her *O virtus Sapientiae* (O strength of wisdom):

O virtus sapientiae, lumen cordium revelans,

Rivus inenarrabilis, flammae dulcissimae.

[O power (or strength) of wisdom, revealing the light of hearts, ineffable stream, sweetest flame.]

Her Latin floated like a mist, weaving through the candlelight. Gödel sat enraptured, hearing not only the notes but also the urge behind them. Each phrase felt like a question and an answer blended—a pattern that hovered on the edge of something ineffable.

When she paused, the silence weighed heavily, as though the air itself mourned that any sound should ever end, like demanding recursiveness. Gödel stood, drawing in a slow breath.

"In my theorems, I found that every formal system has statements that, while true, cannot be proven within the system. Yet I can see their truth from the outside. Your melody does something similar: It suggests an order, a harmony, which surpasses the written notes." He pointed at the music she held in her hand; the parchment was covered in neumes—little squiggles indicating pitch and rhythm. "No neume can fully enclose the living sound."

Hildegard's eyes glowed. "You know something of my secret," she said. "The neumes guide, but they do not govern. They are marks upon parchment, yet when I sing, the sound travels beyond every mark. The rules of counterpoint taught by the monks at Saint Gall give structure, yet I often feel the melody spring from truth untaught—like a fountain rising from the ground. The flute and the psaltery accompany me, but only because I need their texture, their resonance, to carry the vision to those whose ears cannot hear the direct voice of the angels."

BEYOND THE MONASTERY WALLS

As dawn bloomed into morning, the other sisters gathered in the choir. Some hummed bits of chant; others tuned the psalteries and hammered the small cymbal-like cymbala. Hildegard motioned Gödel toward a small lectern where she kept a leather-bound book: *Scivias*, the record of her first twenty-six visions. The pages, with vivid wheels of color, strange creatures, and concentric circles, seemed to pulse with divine rhythm.

"Here," she said, "I wrote down the forms I saw. In one vision, I beheld a great wheel rotating, its spokes radiating like lotus petals. I interpreted it as the entirety of creation, held together by God's will. Yet no ink, however vibrant, can convey the living fire I witnessed."

Gödel reached out, turning a folio gently. He studied the diagrams: wheels within wheels, concentric spheres representing heaven, earth, and the human soul. He thought of how, in his notebooks, he sketched the encodings—Gödel numbers—that mapped statements onto integers. Here, Hildegard's wheels were also mappings of spiritual truths onto geometric forms. He felt a surge of kinship: her visions in art; his arithmetic logic.

"My theorems imply that no system can capture every truth about arithmetic. Your visions show that no manuscript can capture every dimension of the divine. In both cases," he said, "the map cannot be the territory. Yet the map is necessary, for without it, we have no share in the realm beyond."

Hildegard nodded, her eyes misting. "I fear that many in the church distrust what I write. Some say, 'But you are a woman—how can you know such things?' Yet, I believe that any soul, if attuned, can receive these revelations. The sisters copy, the scribes illustrate, but the origin is higher than any hand that holds a quill."

THE THRESHOLD OF INCOMPLETENESS

Beyond the enclosed cloister lay the world of politics and war. Reports had come from Emperor Frederick's court: dissension, prayers answered and unanswered, perhaps hinting at the great mysteries that shaped human destiny. Hildegard often warned rulers through her letters—letters that some whispered were too bold for a woman cloistered behind stone. The period of the Holy Roman Empire during the twelfth century was one of turbulent political and religious climate, specifically during the reign of Emperor Frederick I Barbarossa (reigned 1155–1190). This period deeply shaped Hildegard von Bingen's life and works.

Gödel, too, had faced suspicion. His ideas, though revolutionary, unsettled many who clung to the dream of a perfectly consistent mathematics: Russell, Hilbert, as well as others. To them, a complete, all-encompassing system was the pinnacle. But Gödel's proof shattered that ideal. Now, in this twelfth-century monastery, he felt that Hildegard's music offered a parallel shattering of complacency: a reminder that the realm of spirit always exceeds the boundaries of any rule.

He closed his eyes, hearing again her chant echoing off the stone arches. When he spoke, his voice was soft but firm.

"Abbess Hildegard, if a truth exists *beyond* the formal—be it mathematical or spiritual—how does one live in a world bound by rules? Must we choose between formal logic and divine vision?"

Hildegard's lips curved in a gentle smile. She placed her hand on a chalice resting on the altar—a simple vessel of hammered silver. "No, dear friend. We dwell in *both* worlds. You use axioms from *outside* when you prove a theorem. I use visions from *outside* when I compose a chant. In both, we acknowledge the incompleteness: that each day's chant must end, that each proof must rest on an unprovable axiom."

Gödel's breath felt full. In his quiet solitude back in Princeton, he had once wondered whether the universe itself was akin to a formal system—explicable if only one could find the right axioms. But Hildegard's presence here, her music vibrating through the stone, showed him a different way to reconcile. Perhaps mathematics and mysticism were not so distant after all.

A HARMONY OF ENDS AND BEGINNINGS

As the sun climbed higher, golden light flooded through the chapel's stained-glass windows, illuminating Hildegard's face as she lifted another chant from the psalter. Gödel felt time slip—a strange sensation for one so accustomed to precise chronology. Moments stretched, folded back on themselves, like a fugue whose subject kept returning in unexpected keys.

"Before I depart," Gödel said gently, "tell me: What do you hope for your music? Do you wish it to last forever?"

Hildegard placed a palm over her heart. "Music lives in the present moment. When the sisters raise their voices, time stands still. But every sung note fades. And yet, in that fading, I trust it has reached beyond—to the place where no parchment can follow. That, to me, is eternity."

Gödel understood wholeheartedly. The theorems he proved were bound to the pens he used; he could show that arithmetic would never be complete. Yet he also believed that in recognizing a truth outside any system—an intuition, a vision—he touched something eternal. He bowed his head.

"Then I shall carry your music with me," he whispered. "When I return, I will remember that every formal proof needs a source—just as your music needs the breath of angels. I thank you, abbess, for teaching me that *limit is not limitation, but invitation*."

Hildegard inclined her head once more, as though blessing him. The sisters began to chant again, a gentle wave of sound that seemed to cradle the ancient stones. A soft wind rustled outside the chapel doors, as if the world itself exhaled in concord.

And so, in that Benedictine monastery—caught between vision and reason—two seekers from distant domains found that the air of wonder need not be owned by either faith or logic alone. In Hildegard's melodies and in Gödel's proofs lay a shared longing: to glimpse the vast tapestry that enfolds all finite creations, whether notes on parchment or theorems on paper.

In that hushed dawn, their dialogue became another layer in the grand, unfinished symphony of human striving toward the infinite.

CHAPTER ELEVEN

THE DRIP OF INFINITY

—Jackson Pollock

Creativity is the ability to introduce order into the randomness of nature.

—ERIC HOFFER

GÖDEL STEPPED OFF THE SUBWAY into Manhattan's sultry spring air, the city humming with restless energy both foreign and familiar. He had come to New York to present his latest thoughts on formal logic at a symposium, yet an unplanned detour down a narrow side street had thrust him before Peggy Guggenheim's Art of This Century gallery. Its glass doors glowed like a threshold to another realm—an invitation too compelling to resist.

Inside, the cavernous white room throbbed with Jackson Pollock's drip paintings—canvases laid flat on the floor, each vibrating with looping lines and splattered pigments. Gödel's first glance spurred a shiver of wonder. These images defied neat boundaries, as though the paint itself resisted containment. He approached a colossal work of black, brown, and ochre sinews, murmuring, "An undecidable sentence," and thought of his 1931 theorems that proved certain truths would forever lie beyond any system's reach.

A gallery attendant materialized at his elbow, offering a slender magnifier on a ribbon. "It's like watching chaos make sense of itself," she said. "But what does it mean?"

Gödel nodded. "That is the question." He wondered whether Pollock, in flinging paint, encoded an objective law of beauty, or whether each spectator rewrote the meaning anew with every fresh pair of eyes.

"Dr. Gödel?" she said conspiratorially, as if having a hint of the weight of who Gödel was. "Aren't you the master of unresolved incompleteness? I think you'd delight in seeing the infinities within these drips." Under the lens, a single droplet of cadmium red unraveled into endless tendrils, evoking the fractals Mandelbrot had mapped just a decade earlier.

Gödel lingered, entranced. Then, a friendly voice broke his concentration. "Lost in the loops?" Turning, he saw Peggy Guggenheim, elegant in a midnight-blue gown. "These paintings," she said, "are a dialogue between painter and canvas."

Gödel studied the drips. "A dialogue," he echoed. "Every drop demands interpretation?"

Just then, Pollock himself emerged—tall and restless—his boots leaving faint smudges on the gallery floor. Peggy guided him forward. "Jackson, this is Kurt Gödel," Peggy introduced. "He showed the world that no formal system can prove all its truths."

She then pointed to Pollock. "Meet the man who paints the unseen."

Pollock inclined his head. "I want the painting to surprise me," he confessed. "I set the stage, then surrender." Pollock smiled, tipping his cap. "I am delighted to meet you, Herr Gödel. You humble me with your presence."

Pollock stepped to the edge of a canvas, palms open toward its surface. "This one started with a fall of liquid paint but then became its own world. You can't catch the first stroke without unleashing a thousand more."

Gödel nodded, excitement igniting. "In logic, once axioms are laid, we derive theorems—but find statements neither provable nor disprovable. Your paintings mirror that—they're proofs that never conclude."

"I chase the order hidden inside disorder," said Pollock. "The canvas holds an infinity of possibilities until the last drop hits the floor."

Jackson Pollock was born January 28, 1912, in Cody, Wyoming, and found his artistic calling after studying under Thomas Hart Benton at New York's Art Students League. By 1947, he had revolutionized painting with his drip technique, splattering enamel paints across canvases. Early reactions ranged from bafflement to outright hostility. In 1947, a critic in *Art News* dismissed his work as "mere chaos on canvas," while some contemporaries scoffed that he was simply flinging paint at a floor. Yet a smaller coterie hailed Pollock as an American pioneer, a visionary forging a new path.

The turning point came in August 1949, when *Life* magazine published a story titled "Jackson Pollock: Is He the Greatest Living Painter in the United States?" and introduced his work to millions. Suddenly, his canvases were no longer curiosities but symbols of postwar innovation, later being labeled "Jack the Dripper." Collectors clamored for his paintings, museums queued to exhibit them, and Pollock's name became synonymous with abstract expressionism.

By the mid-1950s, the initial shock had given way to admiration. Audiences marveled at the physicality of his "action painting," recognizing his canvases as choreographed performances immortalized in pigment. Scholars began analyzing his fractal-like structures decades later, confirming what viewers once intuited: These works were not chaos; they contained complexity on par with nature's own patterns.

Figure 12. Jackson Pollock painting in his studio, 1950. Photograph by © 1991 Hans Namuth Estate, courtesy Center for Creative Photography, University of Arizona (AAE Portal)

PAINTING AS PROOF, EXPANDED DIALOGUE

Reinvigorated by Pollock's presence, Gödel paced before a sprawling canvas. Pollock invited him to dip a slender rod into the paint. Hesitant at first, Gödel made a single drip. The pigment splashed—its irregular trajectory was both random and deliberate.

"See?" Pollock said softly. "Every drop responds to the last. You shape it, but you let it shape you."

"So, art's objectivity and the viewer's subjectivity collaborate." Gödel gestured at the canvas. "Exactly. The painting asserts a structure—its composition, rhythm, balance—yet remains open ended. Its meaning completes only when an *observer* engages, projecting their algorithms onto it." He paused. "Theory and reality meet and transform each other.

Gödel cradled the rod, reflecting aloud: "In a formal proof, each inference follows logically, yet the total system cannot capture every truth within. The beginning axiom seems simple, yet the consequences run infinitely deep, just like your paint."

"Logic and paint," Pollock mused, "both dance around the unknown."

Peggy leaned in. "Critics once called Jackson's work formless. Now they see geometry in his chaos. Maybe logic needs a little disorder too."

THE INFINITE WITHIN ACTION

Invited to sit at a low café table out back, they sipped dark espresso. Gödel sketched nested loops on a napkin. "Imagine a painting that writes its own commentary," he said, "each hue annotating the last stroke."

Pollock grinned. "A proof that paints itself."

Gödel sketched a swirling loop in his notebook, mirroring

Pollock's lines. Beneath it, he wrote:

A system's beauty lies not in its closure, but in its invitation to transcend itself.

He closed his eyes and saw Pollock's voids fill with infinite possibility—a fractal universe forever expanding. And he knew that art and logic were not rivals but companions on the same quest: to map the unknown, embrace its surprises, and find, in that interplay, the enduring thrill of discovery.

Gödel said, "Like Escher's *Drawing Hands*." He tapped the napkin. "And viewers become coauthors, interpreting and extending the theorem. What if mathematics and art held symposia together?"

Pollock's eyes gleamed. "I'd love to see mathematicians messy with paint and painters lost in equations. Society may not know what to do with the consequences."

As evening settled, Gödel asked more profound questions about the gallery's reception over time. Peggy recounted how early audiences recoiled at Pollock's seeming disregard for form, only to later embrace his canvases as revolutionary statements on human agency and chance. She noted letters from veterans who saw echoes of their chaotic memories in Pollock's rocky surfaces and critics who, decades later, studied the fractal dimensions of his works to quantify their innate complexity.

Gödel reflected, "Your art acknowledges both the necessity of structure—choosing a canvas, selecting pigments—and the inevitability of the unforeseen—gravity, drips, human movement. It is meta-logic incarnate."

Pollock placed a hand on Gödel's shoulder. "Maybe your theorems and my drips are siblings—born from the same quest to map the uncontainable."

CONVERGENCE AND DEPARTURE

They reconvened before the largest canvas, now under soft spotlights. Gödel breathed deeply, as though inhaling the painting's essence. "I've learned something vital today," he said. "That understanding can be both rigorous and open ended—proof and possibility intertwined."

Pollock nodded solemnly. "That's art."

Outside, New York's skyline beckoned like a constellation of open questions. As Gödel descended the gallery stairs, he carried with him a new metaphor: the act of inquiry as an ongoing performance, each stroke of thought echoing indefinitely.

Later, alone in his hotel room, Gödel placed a small slip of paper in his notebook:

Let the proof spill like paint. Let the canvas breathe chance. In every droplet, find an abyss—and step within.

He smiled, imagining future chapters—dialogues with musicians, sculptors, and writers—all exploring the dance between order and oblivion. And as the city lights shimmered beyond his window, he realized that in art as in logic, the dance never ends—it merely invites the next participant to join.

SECTION III

PHILOSOPHY, ETHICS, AND MORALITY

CHAPTER TWELVE

THE DEATH OF CERTAINTY

—Socrates

The unexamined life is not worth living.

—SOCRATES

A FLICKERING OIL LAMP dimly lit the cell. Shadows danced along the stone walls, twisting into uncertain forms. Kurt Gödel stood in the doorway, his breath steady but his mind racing. This was not a dream—not like the other encounters. This was something else. Something more.

Seated in the center of the room, cross-legged on a small cot, was the man he had come to see. Socrates. Renowned for his integrity, probing intellect, and the development of the Socratic method—a form of cooperative dialogue based on asking and answering questions—he challenged conventional beliefs and encouraged critical self-examination.

The great philosopher's wrists were unshackled—his captors did not believe chains were necessary for a man who would not run. His expression was serene, yet his eyes burned with the same intensity that had made Athens both admire and fear him. The same eyes that had led men to offer him hemlock rather than listen to the truth.

Gödel stepped forward and spoke in a quiet but firm voice. "I have traveled far to speak with you, Socrates. My name is Kurt Gödel, born very long after your time."

The philosopher smiled, his head tilting slightly. "Then you are fortunate, my friend. For time is something I now have in abundance—until I do not."

THE PHILOSOPHER'S FATE

Gödel studied him. The calm, the composure—it unsettled him. "Do you truly accept this fate? To die for asking questions?"

Socrates spread his hands. "Would you have me fight it? Would you have me rage against the men who fear what they do not understand?"

Gödel hesitated. "Yes. That is exactly what I would have you do. The mind is sacred. To silence it is to silence the one thing that can make sense of the world."

Socrates chuckled, his voice warm yet resolute. "Ah, my friend. But you know as well as I that *truth is rarely welcomed by those in power*. I have done only what I was meant to do. To question. To probe. To hold up a mirror to men who do not wish to see themselves. And for that, they offer me poison. So be it."

Gödel clenched his fists. He had spent his life proving that truth itself had limits, that there were things even reason could not reach. And yet, here was a man who had embraced the search for truth with such conviction that he would rather die than cease his questioning.

"But surely you see the injustice of it," Gödel pressed. "Surely you understand that this is not just the death of a man but of reason itself."

Socrates leaned forward. "And yet, here you are, centuries later, still asking questions. Have they silenced reason, then?"

Gödel exhaled. "No. But they have done their best. And they will continue to do so. *Those who seek certainty will always resent those who ask questions.*"

Socrates smiled. "Then let them resent us. For *certainty is the comfort of those unwilling to think*. And thinking—ah, thinking is a dangerous thing."

FROM SOCRATES TO ARISTOTLE TO GÖDEL

Gödel sat on the edge of a worn wooden stool. "I've been recently studying the works of Aristotle—he was the most famous student of Plato, your student. Yet, in many ways he broke from his teacher's ideas. Plato taught that the deepest truths about reality exist in a perfect, eternal realm beyond the physical world—the world of forms or ideas—and that what we see around us is only an imperfect copy of those ideals. Aristotle, while respecting Plato, took a different view. He argued that truth and knowledge are found by studying the world we live in directly. Instead of looking to a separate, unseen realm, Aristotle believed that reality exists here and now, embedded in the physical things themselves. By observing nature, examining causes, and using reason, we can understand reality. He believed that truth could be grasped, that reality itself was embedded in the structure of things."

Socrates nodded. "Aristotle seems like a great thinker, but he may wish for knowledge to be tidy and ordered. I fear he would have found my method too unruly. But tell me, what do you think? Can truth ever be fully grasped?"

Gödel hesitated. "No. I have shown—mathematically—that even within the most rigorous logical systems, there are truths that cannot be proven from within the system itself. Knowledge, no matter how structured, is incomplete. There will always be truths beyond our reach. Beyond the system."

Socrates's eyes gleamed. "Then it seems we are not so different, you and me. For what is my method—my Socratic questioning—if not an admission that knowledge is always incomplete? That every answer births another question?"

Gödel sat back, feeling the weight of Socrates's words. He had spent his life proving the limits of knowledge. And yet, here sat the man who had embodied those limits, who had turned ignorance into the foundation of wisdom.

"And yet," Gödel said softly, "you would still ask questions, even knowing that some answers will forever be out of reach?"

Socrates laughed. "Of course. What else is a mind for? *To know one's ignorance is the beginning of all wisdom.* Tell me, Gödel—would you stop seeking simply because you cannot know all?"

Gödel shook his head. "No. Never."

Socrates clapped his hands. "Then you have understood me better than most! You must write about this, Gödel. Tell the world that questioning is not a means to an end—it is the end itself. Knowledge is never finished. And those who believe they have reached certainty have only ceased thinking."

A FINAL REQUEST

Gödel felt something shift within him—a realization he had not yet fully articulated. "Then what should I tell them, Socrates? If I am to write of you, if I am to carry your thoughts forward, what must I say?"

Socrates smiled, his gaze steady. "Tell them that *knowledge is the great journey, not the final destination.* That to know is not to arrive but to walk endlessly forward. Tell them that reason is a gift, but it is not enough. It must be accompanied by wonder, by humility. And tell them this: Truth, in the deepest sense, is not found in conclusions but in the courage to never stop searching."

Gödel swallowed. The weight of those words pressed upon him. "I will."

Socrates nodded. "Then I am content."

A noise echoed down the stone corridor—the sound of footsteps, slow and deliberate. The guards were coming. Socrates stood, adjusting his robe as though he were merely preparing for an evening walk.

Gödel felt an ache in his chest. "This is wrong."

Socrates placed a hand on his shoulder. "Perhaps. But if my death inspires even one man to think, then it is worth it. And here you are, thinking. Questioning. That is enough."

Figure 13. *The Death of Socrates* (1790). Source: Met Open Access Initiative (public domain artworks).

The door creaked open. The guard stepped forward.

"It is time."

Socrates turned back to Gödel, smiling. "Now, my friend, go. Think. Question. And never let them tell you that knowledge has an end."

Gödel wanted to say something, anything, but his throat was tight. Instead, he nodded, watching as Socrates walked forward, unshaken, into the certainty of his fate.

The door closed.

And the search for truth continued.

CHAPTER THIRTEEN

THE WAGER OF THE HEART

—Pascal

All of humanity's problems stem from man's inability to sit quietly in a room alone.

—BLAISE PASCAL

THE WAVES ROLLED GENTLY onto the shore, their rhythmic movement blending with the distant cries of gulls drifting along the wind. The Mediterranean stretched endlessly before Kurt Gödel, who sat alone on a wooden bench along the promenade, gazing at the horizon. The ocean's vastness unsettled him in a way that only infinite things could—there was always more beyond, always something unknowable just past the reach of his mind.

He had come here, to the South of France, seeking respite, though rest never came easily to a mind preoccupied with incompleteness. Perhaps it was the warm breeze, the way it carried the scent of salt and lavender, that lulled him into reverie. Perhaps it was the slow cadence of the tides that set his thoughts adrift, wandering past formal logic and into something more elusive. The limits of knowledge, of mathematics, of certainty itself—these thoughts never left him.

"It is an extraordinary sight, is it not?" A voice interrupted his contemplation.

Gödel turned to see a man standing nearby, dressed in attire that seemed somewhat anachronistic—dark wool despite the warmth, with an air of old-world elegance. The man had a sharp, intelligent gaze, a certain intensity in his expression that Gödel found familiar.

"Yes," Gödel replied cautiously, as if not fully convinced he had left his own thoughts. "The ocean. An endless expanse, and yet it follows laws we barely grasp."

The stranger smiled. "Indeed. The very forces that govern the ocean's waves govern the heavens above. A grand symmetry in the design of things."

Gödel studied him, something about the man stirring a recognition within him. "You speak as if you see the order in all things. May I ask your name?"

The man extended his hand with a slight bow. "Blaise Pascal."

Gödel hesitated for a moment, then shook his hand, not entirely surprised. If ever there was a man he had wished to meet, even beyond the limits of time, it was Pascal.

PASCAL: THE BRIDGE BETWEEN REASON AND FAITH

Blaise Pascal (1623–1662) lived in seventeenth-century France—born in the provinces (Clermont) and later drawn into the growing intellectual life of Paris and Rouen. A mathematician, physicist, and philosopher, he laid the first stones of probability, probed the behavior of fluids and pressure, and built one of the earliest calculating machines to help his father. A man of astonishing intellect, his life was cut short by stomach cancer—he was only thirty-nine when he succumbed to it.

Figure 14. Blaise Pascal, line engraving after G. Edelinck after F. Quesnel, Jr. Source: Clermont Auvergne Métropole, Bibliothèque du patrimonine, GRA 6025 (public domain).

Beyond his scientific contributions, he was a thinker tormented by the weight of existence itself. In his later years, he turned from experiments to questions that stretched past mathematics—questions of faith, of meaning, and of the limits of human reason.

Gödel had always admired Pascal's mind, not only for his rigorous approach to mathematical truth but for his willingness to engage with the ineffable. Where most scientists sought certainty, Pascal had accepted uncertainty.

"Pascal's wager," Gödel mused. "A bet on faith itself. If one must choose between belief in God and disbelief, and the stakes are infinite, then reason demands we believe. For to wager on disbelief and be wrong is to lose everything."

Pascal nodded. "It is not purely a wager, you see. It is the recognition that *reason alone cannot take us where we must go.*"

Gödel considered this. "And yet, you were also a mathematician. Did it never trouble you to place such weight on something beyond logic?"

Pascal smiled. "Not at all. If anything, it was mathematics that led me there. I saw in numbers and in probability the same reality I saw in faith—a structure, a certainty, even when the conclusion itself was unseen."

GÖDEL AND THE LIMITS OF KNOWLEDGE

"Incompleteness," Gödel said, half to himself. "Even in mathematics, there are truths that can never be proven from within the system. There are limits to what we can know, no matter how refined our logic."

"Precisely," Pascal said, his eyes lighting up. "And this is what the mind must accept. We stand on the precipice of knowledge, seeing just enough to understand that there is more—infinitely more—beyond our grasp."

Gödel turned back to the sea. "I have spent my life proving that knowledge has boundaries. No system or framework of human reasoning can encapsulate all truths. And yet, I struggle with what that means. Does it imply something beyond knowledge itself? Something external to reason?"

Pascal placed a hand on the wooden railing. "It implies that reason is a tool, not the final destination. Mathematics and science are lenses through which we glimpse reality, but they are not reality itself."

Gödel let out a quiet laugh. "Then we are all blind men describing an elephant, touching only fragments of truth."

"And yet," Pascal countered, "we touch enough to know that the elephant is real."

FAITH AND THE GRAND DESIGN

They sat in silence for a while, watching the endless movement of the waves. Finally, Gödel spoke. "If knowledge is limited, then faith is required to fill the gaps. But faith in what?"

Pascal leaned back. "Faith in order. In the unseen structure that holds the cosmos together. You see, my friend, *faith is not opposed to reason*—it is what allows reason to function at all. Without it, there would be no axioms to mathematics, no assumptions upon which logic is built. We put our trust in those first principles, even though we cannot prove them."

Gödel thought for a moment. "Then perhaps faith is woven into the very fabric of existence. Not just in theology, but in science itself."

Pascal smiled. "Exactly. The question is not whether we have faith, but *where we place it*."

The sun dipped lower toward the horizon, casting golden streaks across the water. The conversation had taken them far, yet it felt as though they had only begun.

Gödel exhaled, feeling a rare sense of peace. "It seems there is no escaping the infinite. Whether in numbers or in the cosmos, it is always there."

Pascal nodded. "And perhaps that is the greatest proof of all."

As the evening tide began to roll in, the two men continued

their conversation, their minds grappling with the mysteries that had occupied thinkers for centuries. Though they approached from different angles—one from the rigor of logic, the other from the embrace of faith—they found themselves standing at the same threshold, gazing into the vast, endless unknown.

CONTINUATION: THE SOUL OF MATHEMATICS AND THE HIDDEN ORDER

Pascal gestured toward the horizon. "You know, monsieur, mathematics itself is a reflection of something deeper. It is as if the universe has been written in numbers, in patterns, in ratios that are too perfect to be accidental. The golden ratio, the Fibonacci sequence, the structure of the cosmos—these hint at something grander than mere chance."

Gödel nodded. "Yes, and yet we cannot prove that mathematics itself is complete. There will always be something outside our reach. Perhaps, as you suggest, we are only reading fragments of a divine manuscript."

Gödel leaned back, his eyes reflecting the twinkling horizon. "Then perhaps it is the gaps—the unprovable, the unknown—that allow beauty to exist. Like the silent pauses in a symphony, these intervals create the space for wonder, for imagination, for faith."

Pascal's lips curved into a warm, knowing smile. "Indeed. Imagine if every note in life were predetermined by cold logic. The melody of our existence would be bereft of its most enchanting variations. It is in our willingness to embrace mystery, to wager on that unseen order, that we find our true freedom."

The two men sat side by side, their thoughts mingling with the salty breeze. As the sun finally sank below the ocean's edge, casting long shadows and a soft, forgiving glow, Gödel's mind wandered to the paradox of certainty and uncertainty. "In mathematics, as in life, we reach for truths that always elude our grasp. Yet, in that very elusiveness, there is an *invitation*—a dare to dream beyond the boundaries of proof."

Pascal laughed gently, a sound that mingled with the whisper of the waves. "And what a delightful wager it is, my friend! To bet not on what can be rigorously demonstrated but on the serendipity of the heart. For every theorem left unproven, there lies an endless realm of possibility. We are both scholars and adventurers, navigating a cosmos where every unknown is a door waiting to be opened."

As twilight deepened, the stars began to punctuate the sky—a silent reminder of the infinite questions above. Gödel and Pascal rose from the bench, their conversation lingering like a cherished secret between reason and faith. With a final glance at the ever-expanding sea of mysteries, they stepped forward together into the night, their steps light and their hearts buoyed by the promise that in every unanswered question, there lay a universe of wonder waiting to be embraced.

CHAPTER FOURTEEN

REASON'S EDGE

—Kant

I have therefore found it necessary to deny knowledge in order to make room for faith.

—IMMANUEL KANT (from *Critique of Pure Reason*, which makes the case for rational faith)

Kurt Gödel didn't fear madness. He feared unreality—the creeping suspicion that behind the bright wallpaper of facts and figures, there was nothing but smoke.

He often sat in his study in Princeton, coat buttoned even in summer, poring not only over mathematics but philosophy—Leibniz, Plato, Edmund Husserl, and Immanuel Kant. What he wanted to know wasn't just what is true but how we know anything is true at all—old-fashioned epistemology.

Kant distrusted the body. The senses could be deceived—hallucinations, mirages, faulty instruments. But he also began to suspect the mind. Logic, once thought to be the unbreakable ladder to truth, had shown its limits.

Gödel's incompleteness theorems proved that even arithmetic—the purest domain of reason—harbored statements that were true but forever unprovable within the system itself.

If logic had blind spots, what could be trusted?

Gödel's thoughts swirled like snow—slow, silent, persistent—until one evening, as twilight draped itself across his study and the outside world dimmed into abstraction, he closed his eyes.

And opened them in a different world.

A snow-dusted grove.

Silent but not empty.

Light came from nowhere and everywhere, casting no shadows. The trees stood like axioms—spaced, unchanging, dignified.

From a distance, a figure approached along a narrow path that seemed too perfect to have formed by chance.

It was Immanuel Kant (1724–1804)—precise, composed, eyes deep with structured thought. He carried the air of a man who had once built a fortress out of reason to defend the trembling kingdom of knowledge.

Figure 15. Anonymous engraving based on an anonymous painting. Source: Wikimedia Commons (public domain).

Gödel rose to meet him.

"You look exactly as I imagined," Gödel said quietly.

"And you," Kant replied, "sound exactly as I feared."

They walked together—one careful, one ethereal—as philosophers from different centuries but on the same battlefield.

"I have been thinking," Gödel said, "about knowing. About how we move from belief to knowledge, and how frail that bridge really is."

Kant nodded. "You are not the first to doubt the senses. Descartes suspected a demon. Hume drowned in skepticism."

"And you tried to rescue us."

"I tried to rescue reason," Kant corrected. "By redefining its domain. I did not prove we could know things as they are. Only how they appear to us."

"Phenomena," Gödel said.

"Yes. Structured by the mind's own machinery—space, time, causality, quantity, modality. We do not see space and time; we think in them *(inside the system)*. They are not out there but in here." He tapped his temple.

Gödel considered this. "So, what we call reality is always filtered. Categorized."

Kant smiled faintly. "There is no raw access. The noumenal world—things in themselves—remains forever beyond us. We cannot know it. We can only know what our mind makes of it."

Gödel bent to pick up a piece of snow—perfectly formed, unmelted by touch. "But what if the truth lies in the noumenal? What if the most important things are precisely what we cannot reach?"

"Then," Kant said, "we are creatures who live by faith, though we speak in reason."

They walked on.

"You set boundaries for knowledge," Gödel said. "And I, by accident, found a hole in the floorboards. Something transcendent; *outside the system.*" He leaned forward. "What I discovered is that in any logical system—any system built on rules, like mathematics—there are always some true statements that can't be proven using only the rules inside that system. No matter how carefully you set up the rules, there will always be questions that those rules alone cannot answer. My theorems show that human knowledge and logic have built-in limits—there will always be mysteries that go beyond any list of rules we create."

Kant nodded slowly. "Your theorems say that even within formal systems—mathematics, logic—there are propositions that are true, yet unprovable? That is no small crack. That is an earthquake beneath the Enlightenment."

"It means," Gödel said, "that truth outruns proof. That knowing requires something more than deduction. An intuition. A leap."

Kant stopped. "Then you see why I turned to morality. To freedom. Not as empirically provable but as rational necessities. I could not prove God, but I believed we must act as if he exists. For law, for meaning, for the self to be free. For living life pragmatically." Kant had written a treatise, *Critique of Practical Reason* (1788), in which he concluded that while theoretical reason cannot provide knowledge of God, freedom, or immortality, practical reason requires us to postulate these ideas as *necessary assumptions for moral life.*

Gödel's eyes narrowed. "But if morality isn't grounded in logic . . . then what?"

Kant raised a hand and pointed upward.

"Two things," he said, "fill the mind with ever-increasing wonder and awe: the starry heavens above, and the moral law within."

Gödel looked up. The sky above the grove shimmered—not with stars but with pure forms. Equations, or perhaps prayers, moving without motion.

"You said reason must be confined to make room for faith," Gödel said. "But *what if reason itself, at its edge, is faith?*"

Kant nodded slowly. "Then perhaps our greatest knowledge is not certainty—but humility."

A clearing opened before them. In its center stood a mirror. Yet it reflected no faces—only questions.

Gödel stepped closer. "I once wrote a formal proof for the existence of God. Based on modal logic. It was elegant. Precise."

"Did it satisfy you?" Kant asked.

"No," Gödel said. "Because even that proof lives inside a system. And all systems, I have learned, are incomplete."

They stood together—the moralist and the logician—not as opposites but as companions at the edge of knowability. One built the frame; the other saw the cracks. Both knew that knowledge without limits becomes hubris, and doubt without ground becomes despair.

Kant looked into the mirror. "Maybe God is the noumenon. The unknowable that makes knowing possible."

Gödel replied, barely above a whisper, "Maybe meaning isn't something we discover. Maybe it's something we *receive*."

As they turned to part, Gödel paused.

"In Ecclesiastes," he said, "Solomon tried everything—wisdom, wealth, pleasure, toil—and found it all chasing after the wind."

"Yes," Kant said, eyes distant. "And yet he concluded: 'Fear God and keep his commandments, for this is the whole duty of man.' Not provable. Not rational in the Enlightenment sense. But perhaps the deepest form of knowledge is reverence."

The wind stirred, though nothing moved. The snow did not melt, did not fall. It simply was.

Kant turned, walking back down the path, precise as ever.

Gödel remained, looking into the mirror one last time. No answers appeared. Only the quiet truth that some questions are not meant to be solved—only carried.

And in that moment, he felt something strange.

Not certainty.

But peace.

CHAPTER FIFTEEN

FREEDOM'S RECKONING

—Sartre

Life has no meaning the moment you lose the illusion of being eternal.
—JEAN-PAUL SARTRE (reflecting on the human confrontation with mortality and the meaning of existence)

IT BEGAN IN A TRANCE—not strange because it defied logic but because it revealed too much. As Gödel sat immersed in notes on ethics and the limits of formal systems, the lamplight dimmed and the air thickened. The pages of *Principia Mathematica* (not Newton's but Bertrand Russell's) stirred as though disturbed by memory. That volume, once a symbol of humankind's dream to contain all truth within logic, had long since become, for him, a reminder of our limits. Its ambitions were noble, yet they cracked beneath the weight of truths that could not be proved. In that moment, as if summoned by the silent protest of incompleteness, the walls of the study dissolved, and Gödel stood in a place beyond dates—beyond time itself.

What is left when even logic admits its insufficiency? That question had lingered with him for years. Just as no mathematical system could affirm all its own truths, no human conscience, left solely to itself, seemed capable of safeguarding meaning against corruption. Gödel often wondered: If a formal system breaks under the weight of its own limitations, what then of an existential one—built not on numbers but on *choice*? It was in that contemplation, hovering between theorem and conscience, that the space around him began to change.

In the quiet chambers of his mind, Gödel staged an imaginary encounter with Jean-Paul Sartre (1905–1980). He pictured them in a bustling Parisian symposium—Sartre, animated and resolute, arguing that human beings are condemned to be free, that meaning is not found but made. In this mental theater, Gödel listened intently before replying: No system, whether ethical or logical, can justify its entire structure from within. For true foundations, something must come from beyond the system itself.

Sartre was no ordinary thinker. To many, he was the architect of modern existentialism—a philosophy forged not in abstract speculation but in the crucible of war, occupation, and resistance. He held that there is no predetermined human essence, no divine blueprint; rather, we are what we *choose* to become. In the absence of God or fixed moral law, he believed that meaning arises only from personal commitment, even in absurd or hostile conditions.

His plays and novels, steeped in this defiant freedom, resonated with a generation unmoored from tradition. To Sartre, authenticity was salvation—living in full awareness of one's freedom, even when that freedom was a burden. Yet Gödel wondered: Could this freedom, radical and self-authoring, truly endure the weight of history's most systematic evil?

In the silent landscape of his thoughts, Gödel composed an imaginary letter to Sartre—one never written nor sent in reality. In his mind, he proposed that they carry their philosophical debate beyond the comfort of classrooms and cafés, journeying instead to the ultimate proving ground: Auschwitz. It was there, in this imagined encounter, that Gödel sought to test the limits of their ideas about freedom, meaning, and morality against history's harshest evidence. Could a philosophy of pure will, of self-constructed essence, stand amid the ashes of annihilated persons? To his quiet astonishment, Sartre agreed.

Figure 16. Jean-Paul Sartre (1924). Source: Creative Commons Zero, Public Domain Dedication.

Sartre's reply was steeped in grave sincerity. He acknowledged that his explorations of anguish and authenticity in *La Nausée* could not remain abstractions in the face of the Holocaust. He accepted Gödel's invitation—not as a concession, but as a test. If freedom alone could withstand evil, it would do so there, where evil had taken its most meticulous form.

Jean-Paul Sartre's *La Nausée ("Nausea")* was a landmark existentialist novel that follows Antoine Roquentin, a solitary historian, as he confronts a deep sense of alienation and existential dread in an indifferent world. Sartre's novel captures Roquentin's recurring feelings of revulsion—his nausea—as he comes to realize the banality and emptiness of existence, ultimately recognizing that reality is fundamentally contingent and devoid of inherent meaning. *La Nausée* became a foundational text of existentialist philosophy, powerfully expressing the challenges of human freedom, the search for authenticity, and the confrontation with the absurd.

Gray light seeped through broken barracks as Kurt Gödel and Jean-Paul Sartre arrived at Auschwitz-Birkenau. The morning breeze carried a heavy hush—an absence of life made palpable. Gothic silhouettes of watchtowers rose against a pallid sky, and the railway tracks, once conduits of suffering, lay silent beneath frosted grass. Sartre tugged at his coat, glancing at the iron gates above him. Across his mind flickered memories of *La Nausée*, where his character Roquentin recoiled at the sheer contingency of existence. Yet here, contingency had mutated into systematic horror.

Before they stepped further, Gödel offered a few quiet words: "You have written that existence precedes essence—that we define ourselves through *choice*. But here, essence was imposed: 'Jew,' 'Gypsy,' 'enemy.' No choice. Those labels transformed human beings into objects. Can freedom, as you conceive it, withstand a terror so absolute?"

Sartre crouched by a pair of shattered shoes, brushing dust from a child's slipper. His voice trembled slightly. "In my novel, Roquentin's nausea drives him to affirm his own existence, to choose authenticity. Yet these people were stripped of choice before they could affirm anything. *Freedom requires the space to choose*, and that space here was erased."

They walked onward, past a gate bearing its cruel motto. The slogan seemed a mocking echo of Sartre's own lectures on the responsibilities of freedom.

Gödel paused beside a crumbling wall and spoke carefully: "Imagine morality as a formal system; call it M. You set axioms—'I choose to value life,' 'I reject harm to the innocent'—and derive rules for conduct. My incompleteness theorems demonstrate that some true moral statements cannot be proven within M itself. To recognize them, one must step outside M to an external standard or metasystem. If your only foundation is personal will, it can redefine or dismiss any axiom, including 'murder is wrong.' Only an objective measure—something neither invented nor alterable by individual choice—can enforce nonnegotiable boundaries."

Sartre frowned, folding his arms. "You imply my existential freedom is insufficient, incomplete. Yet I have insisted that appealing to any transcendent standard betrays human responsibility, that we alone must account for our actions."

"Responsibility without foundation can become arbitrary," Gödel replied. "In mathematics, we accept certain axioms—like the basic properties of numbers—without proof, because they lie beyond formal derivation, yet we know they are necessary to build consistent arguments. Morality may demand similar humility: acknowledging that some truths must exist outside our capacity to generate them solely through choice."

They moved past the skeleton remains of a crematorium. Sartre's voice caught in his throat. "I rejected God as an evasion of accountability. But I find that without an anchor beyond the self, nothing prevents will from becoming tyranny. Like Auschwitz."

Gödel placed a gentle hand on Sartre's shoulder. "Admitting limits does not diminish your stance; it deepens it. If you cannot prove every moral truth from within M, you must concede that moral authority rests, in part, on something beyond any one system—perhaps an objective moral order, or at least the recognition that human constructs require external validation."

They reached the "death wall," its pockmarked bricks stained by time. Sartre stared upward, eyes brimming with unshed tears. "I thought that 'hell is other people,' that conflict arises when we objectify each other. Here, I see hell is also us—our freedom perverted into cruelty."

Gödel's voice was firm: "*Freedom without guardrails can destroy itself. True liberty requires constraint.* A constraint not imposed by force alone, but by principle that stands independent of any single will."

They paused beneath a lone birch tree, the ground littered with fragments of memory. Sartre inhaled sharply. "In *La Nausée*, I tried to escape anguish by embracing authenticity—living fully in each moment. But authenticity alone cannot confront horror when horror denies the very possibility of living."

Gödel nodded. "Authenticity, if untethered, becomes solipsism—the absurd notion that only one's own mind is certain to exist, that knowledge outside of one's own consciousness is uncertain and possibly nonexistent. It cannot critique itself. To distinguish life from atrocity, we need an external vantage point—something that transcends personal experience."

Sartre's gaze swept across the ruins as his shoulders slumped. "I admire your willingness to face these limits. I have championed radical freedom as the path to meaningful action. Yet here, meaning itself was weaponized."

Gödel's expression softened. "Your philosophy awakened many to human possibility. But every theory of freedom must answer how it withstands systems that rewrite its own terms. The Holocaust revealed the equal capacity of freedom to create and to annihilate."

They climbed the ramp where countless victims were unloaded. Sartre's steps grew slow, deliberate. "I arrive at a troubling paradox: If I admit a transcendent standard, I risk dogma. If I deny it, I leave no defense against the abyss."

Gödel replied quietly, "Dogma becomes oppressive when it masquerades as full truth. Perhaps we should speak not of dogma but of ground—an acknowledgment that human reasoning has horizons it cannot cross alone. In mathematics, we say, '*We believe these axioms because without them we cannot proceed,*' even though we cannot prove them. Morality may need to begin with a similar prologue: 'We accept certain principles as foundational because our system of freedom demands them.'"

Sartre closed his eyes as though recalling Roquentin's trembling at a café table; now that trembling was magnified hundredfold. He exhaled and whispered, "I . . . I see that my radical freedom, unmoored from any foundation, leads only to despair and complicity. Authenticity rings false when meaning can be perverted."

This was Sartre's dilemma: embrace something beyond the self (transcendence) and risk losing freedom to an external authority or reject it and fall into moral and metaphysical relativism, where anything goes. *Isn't the denial of transcendence itself a dogma*?

Soft sunlight broke through leaden clouds, illuminating the wreckage. Gödel watched it fall across Sartre's face. "We must not forsake freedom; rather, we must seek its ground. Freedom guided by principles that no human will can alter is not less free—it is free to protect itself against its own dark possibilities."

Sartre opened his eyes, a quiet resolve igniting. "I will return from this journey changed. My next work will confront the necessity of ground—of something beyond pure choice—so that freedom can stand as a bulwark against meaninglessness and evil."

Gödel offered a rare gentle smile. "That is proof we both can live with—a testament that inquiry need not end in nihilism but can lead to renewed hope."

They descended the ramp together, leaving behind the echoes of suffering. Each carried the other's questions into a future where freedom and transcendent justice might, for the first time, walk hand in hand.

Over the years that followed, Gödel and Sartre lost touch. Sartre wrestled with the inadequacy he now sensed in his own existentialism and began weaving Marxist elements into his thought—seeking solidarity and the critique of social structures he had once viewed with skepticism. Gödel, learning of his former interlocutor's evolution, wondered whether the weight of Auschwitz had truly settled in Sartre's soul or whether fresh ideologies had offered new axioms to replace old ones.

Gödel believed that some experiences defy reformulation into any system, mathematical or philosophical. The horror they witnessed demanded not only intellectual inquiry but a permanent adhesion to soul and mind. To know is not enough: One must embrace faith in truths beyond proof, allow understanding to take root, and ultimately be changed by them.

In the years that followed, Sartre's steps grew slower, his voice quieter. Blindness stole from him the written word, and with it, the pages upon which he had once built meaning from nothingness. Surrounded by admirers yet encircled by silence, he drifted into a twilight of disillusionment. The revolutions he had once championed curdled into ideology; the freedom he had exalted became a burden too heavy to carry alone. Simone de Beauvoir, his lifelong companion, remained by his side, witnessing the slow unraveling of a man who had once declared the universe absurd and insisted that meaning must be made nonetheless.

In the end, Sartre's philosophy—so bold in its rejection of transcendence—left little to cling to as the body failed and the mind dimmed. And yet, even in that fading, there was a paradox: a life spent chasing authenticity now laid bare by the most unyielding force of all—mortality. Perhaps, in those final silences, he glimpsed what Gödel had long suspected: that freedom without a ground is not liberation, but drift.

Wanting to know is one thing; having faith is another; understanding is still another—but only through transformation do we find redemption.

CHAPTER SIXTEEN

THE MEASURE OF A SOUL

—Faust

Faustus, who embraced evil and shunned righteousness, became the foremost symbol of the misuse of free will and of the tragic consequences that follow from the pursuit of knowledge and power at any cost.

—SAMUEL E. NAVARRO'S reflection on the Faustian archetype

TWILIGHT WRAPPED ITSELF around the old German town, curling through the alleys and cloaking the stones with shadow. Kurt Gödel, lost in thought, wandered aimlessly along the narrow streets, the heavy scent of damp earth and old wood filling the air. In his hands, folded tightly against his chest, was a worn volume—a compilation of folklore and half-remembered histories.

He had been reading about Johann Georg Faust, the man—or myth—whose story had haunted the German imagination for centuries. The brilliant scholar, the restless wanderer, the alchemist who had, it was said, bartered his very soul for a taste of forbidden knowledge and worldly delights. Gödel turned a page slowly, his heart sinking with every word.

Faust had been a man of immense learning, so much so that many said he had surpassed all his contemporaries in medicine, theology, and the arts. But with knowledge came dissatisfaction, and with dissatisfaction, despair. It was said that he found the *limits* of human understanding unbearable—that no matter how many books he devoured, mysteries still yawned beyond his reach. And so, in his impatience, he sought out darker forces, forging a dreadful pact with the devil—for twenty-four years of absolute power and pleasure to be followed by eternal damnation.

Figure 17. Faust and Mephisto enter Auerbach's cellar for the scene of the same name in Goethe's *Faust*. In the foreground, you can see the students drinking (1923). Source: Wikimedia Commons (public domain).

Gödel pressed *The History of Dr. Johann Faust* shut with trembling fingers. The book had been written by an anonymous German author and first published in 1587 by Johann Spies in Frankfurt. Johann Wolfgang von Goethe reimagined it in the nineteenth century and wrote a two-part play that became the magnum opus of German literature.

Faust's tragedy gnawed at Gödel. Faust had not been a fool. He had been brilliant. Yet brilliance had not saved him. Pride, despair, and the terror of limitation had driven him to a fatal choice.

"If only," Gödel whispered to the night, "someone had been there to explain."

He closed his eyes and let the thought unfurl, vivid and painful. What if he had been there? What if, in one decisive conversation, he could have steered Faust from the abyss? Could reason, could truth itself, have stood against the raw hunger that tore at Faust's soul?

The night thickened around him. When he opened his eyes again, the mist had shifted. A crooked inn sign loomed ahead, swinging slowly in the wind—*Zum Schwarzen Raben*. The Black Raven.

As if drawn by an invisible hand, Gödel stepped toward it.

The taproom was dim and low ceilinged, its beams heavy with centuries of soot. Only one figure sat by the hearth, cloaked in velvet and shadow. The fire cast flickering light across his face—a face both young and old, prideful and broken. The man looked up, and a sardonic smile crossed his lips.

"You are late," he said, his voice a dry whisper.

Gödel approached, heart hammering. "Faust?"

"Once," the man replied. "Or perhaps only the idea of him remains."

Gödel sat opposite, his mind awhirl. The book—the story—had become flesh.

"Tell me," Gödel urged. "Why did you do it?"

Faust laughed, a hollow sound that seemed to suck the warmth from the room.

"Because," he said, "I was told there was no boundary I could not cross. No secret I could not unlock. He (the devil) dangled it before me—power, pleasure, knowledge beyond mortal dreams. I was promised everything."

He stared into the fire; the flames reflected in his hollow eyes.

"And what was the price?" Gödel asked gently.

"Everything," Faust whispered. "And I gave it willingly."

Gödel felt a deep ache in his chest. "But why? Why wager your soul?"

Faust's voice rose, trembling with old rage. "Because the soul seemed like a fable! An invisible thing! What weight did it have compared to the gold they poured into my hands? What proof of its worth could the priests and philosophers offer?"

He leaned forward, his face inches from Gödel's.

"Would you not have done the same, logician?"

Gödel held his gaze, unflinching. He recalled Pascal's wager. "No!" he said softly. "Because I have seen—in my work, in my proofs—that not all truths are provable. Not all realities are visible."

Faust sneered. "You would preach to a man who has seen wonders beyond your comprehension?"

"Yes," Gödel said. "Because the wonders you were given were bait. Their brilliance was borrowed, derivative. Like reflections in a tarnished mirror. The true light—the true worth—lies elsewhere."

Faust sagged back in his chair, the anger draining from him. "Explain," he said bitterly. "Explain what I missed."

Gödel drew a deep breath. "In my theorems," he began, "I showed that any consistent system complex enough to contain arithmetic is incomplete. There are truths within it that cannot be proven by its own rules. They require *something outside the system*—an axiom, an insight, a gift."

Faust watched him warily.

"The soul," Gödel continued, "is like that. Worldly measures cannot prove its worth. Not by wealth, not by pleasure, not by knowledge. Its value is a gift, given from outside—by the Creator."

Faust closed his eyes. "I thought I was gaining the world."

"And you lost yourself," Gödel said. "You took the wrong side of Pascal's wager."

For a long time they sat in silence, the fire dwindling to embers.

Finally, Faust spoke, his voice raw. "Is there no redemption for such a fool?"

Gödel's face softened. "Redemption is not earned. It is offered."

Faust's hands trembled as he lifted them, empty, to the darkened rafters. "Then let it be offered," he whispered.

Gödel rose slowly, feeling the enormity of the moment press against him. He reached out and laid a hand on Faust's bowed head.

"You are more than your bargains," he said. "You are more than your sins."

The inn seemed to blur, the walls dissolving into mist. The fire guttered out. When Gödel stepped back into the street, the first light of dawn was breaking, pale and uncertain.

He clutched the worn book to his chest, but he no longer needed its words. The story—the warning of a Faustian bargain—was etched into his mind.

He turned once more toward the empty inn, where no sign now swung, where no door remained.

"Poor Faust," he whispered. "Poor, brilliant, broken Faust."

And he knew—as surely as he knew the paradoxes of mathematics, the mysteries of logic—that the soul's worth is not in its achievements, its pleasures, or its powers. It is not measured at all.

It simply is.

Given. Loved. Eternal.

A truth too often glimpsed only after the wager has been made.

SECTION IV

THEOLOGY AND CHOICE

CHAPTER SEVENTEEN

LONGING AND THE LOGOS

—C. S. Lewis

If I find myself a desire which no experience in this world can satisfy, the most probable explanation is that I was made for another world.

—C. S. LEWIS

Kurt Gödel found himself in Oxford, in a study thick with books and pipe smoke, the scent of old paper mingling with the warm glow of lamplight. The room was cluttered yet inviting—worn leather armchairs, a massive wooden desk strewn with ink-stained pages, and along the far wall, an imposing bookshelf that seemed to stretch into infinity, filled with volumes that looked as though they had been read and reread by minds far greater than his own.

Across from him, seated comfortably with a pipe in hand, was the great thinker and apologist C. S. Lewis. He looked precisely as Gödel had imagined he would—thoughtful but affable, eyes sharp with intellect yet softened by something deeper, something that hinted at experience beyond mere academic pursuit. He exhaled a slow stream of smoke, studying Gödel with a mix of curiosity and amusement.

"You look as though you've wandered in from another world, Herr Gödel," Lewis mused, tapping his pipe against the edge of an ashtray.

Gödel, still adjusting to the surreal nature of his surroundings, managed a small smile. "Perhaps I have. But then, so have you."

Lewis chuckled. "Fair enough. And what brings a mathematician to the company of a storyteller?"

Gödel leaned forward, the weight of the moment pressing on him. "I am aware of your works, Professor Lewis—*Mere Christianity*, *The Great Divorce*, even *The Screwtape Letters*. You were not always a believer in God. You were once like me, devoted to logic and reason, yet unwilling to cross the line into faith. But something changed."

Figure 18. Photograph of undergraduates at University College, Trinity Term 1917 (C. S. Lewis on the right side back row). Source: Wikimedia Commons (public domain).

Lewis studied him, then leaned back, pipe resting between his fingers. "Ah. So, you've come up with the great question."

Gödel nodded. "You were, in a sense, 'converted'—not through blind faith but through reason itself. How does one go from the cold certainty of materialism to belief in a grand designer?"

Lewis smiled as if he had been waiting for this question forever. "Let me tell you a story, then. It begins, as all real stories do, with *doubt*."

The room seemed to shift slightly, the very air thickening with thought as he spoke. "For most of my early life, I was like many intellectuals—suspicious of God, comfortable with the idea that the universe was indifferent, that reason was sufficient to explain all things. But then, a troubling thought took root. If the universe is nothing but atoms and chance, then so is my mind. And if my mind is merely the product of blind material forces, why should I trust it to arrive at the truth? Why should reason itself be valid in a universe that does not care for reason?"

Gödel sat up straighter. "A paradox of logic."

Lewis nodded. "Yes. Then I realized that reason itself is something that should not exist in a purely material world. It is a light that comes from *beyond*. If we trust reason and believe our minds can grasp the truth, then we must accept that there is more to the universe than mere matter."

Gödel exhaled slowly. "Then truth itself is evidence of something beyond."

"Exactly," Lewis said, relighting his pipe. "And so, I found myself walking further and further down a path I had once resisted. But belief is not merely an intellectual exercise. No one converts by reason alone—one must also recognize the nature of the self." He gestured toward a small volume on the desk. "*The Great Divorce*—a story I wrote about souls who travel from a dreary, gray world to a place of light, only to find that they are not yet real enough to exist there."

Gödel's fingers brushed over the book's spine. "A metaphor?"

Lewis smiled. "A reality. We are all unfinished, incomplete. We live in shadows, grasping at meaning but not yet fully real. And to become real, one must recognize *the source* of all reality."

Gödel's mind whirred. "And that source is God."

"Yes," Lewis said. "God is not merely a belief—He is the foundation upon which all logic, all beauty, all truth must stand. Without him, we are left only with contradictions."

Gödel felt a strange, exhilarating sensation, as though he had stumbled upon a hidden proof—one that had always existed but had been waiting for him to see it. "That is the very problem I have encountered in my work. Mathematics, for all its power, has limits. No system is complete in itself—there will always be truths that lie beyond proof, yet they are no less true for being beyond reach." He looked up, meeting Lewis's gaze. "If that is true for mathematics, could it not also be true for the universe?"

Lewis nodded. "You have put it better than I ever could. We are creatures who long for something beyond ourselves. We hunger for meaning, for completion. And that hunger is itself a signpost—it points to something real. Just as a man born with thirst must conclude that water exists, so too must the soul's longing for something greater suggest that such a thing is real."

Gödel's mind reeled, drawing connections between everything he had studied and every paradox he had encountered. "Then those who reject the idea of God are like the souls in *The Great Divorce* who prefer the familiar gray of their own making to the brightness of something beyond."

Lewis's expression grew somber. "Yes. There is a great tragedy in that. Some reject not because they do not see but because they do not wish to see."

A silence fell between them, thick with thought. Gödel glanced at another book on the desk—*The Screwtape Letters*, its cover worn from years of use. "And this? I've wondered about this one—I have not yet read it."

Lewis smirked. "A different sort of study. If one wishes to understand truth, it is wise to understand how lies work as well. Evil does not argue with logic—it distracts, confuses, and whispers in comfortable half truths. It tells men they are already wise enough and need to seek nothing further."

Gödel exhaled. "Then the greatest deception is convincing men that nothing is beyond themselves. The whisper: There is nothing beyond the system. It is the antithesis of wisdom."

Lewis's eyes twinkled. "Precisely."

The clock on the wall ticked softly, the fire crackling in the hearth. Gödel felt something settle in his mind—not an answer, not a proof, but a certainty beyond proof. He had spent his life searching for completeness only to realize that *completeness must lie beyond the system itself.*

Perhaps, he thought, faith was not the abandonment of reason. Perhaps it was its final step.

He rose, offering Lewis his hand. "Thank you."

Lewis shook it firmly. "No, my friend. Thank you for seeking."

The study flickered, the smoke curling into strange spirals. The bookshelves seemed to stretch even farther, their volumes forming endless corridors.

And then—

Gödel awoke.

The air in his study was still, the scent of coffee lingering. His copy of *Mere Christianity* lay open beside him, a passage underlined in ink:

If I find in myself a desire which no experience in this world can satisfy, the most probable explanation is that I was made for another world.

Gödel stared at the words, a slow smile forming. Perhaps, in some strange way, he had just stepped through a door between worlds.

And perhaps, just perhaps, he was finally beginning to see what lay on the other side.

And Gödel, with trembling joy, said: "And now I understand—so that I might believe more deeply."

CHAPTER EIGHTEEN

A DIVINE AXIOM

—Anselm

God is that than which nothing greater can be conceived.

—ANSELM OF CANTERBURY

The air inside Canterbury Cathedral felt thick with eternity. Sunlight spilled through stained-glass windows—blues like a summer sky, reds like fire—and scattered onto stone floors worn smooth by centuries of footsteps and whispered prayers. The hush wasn't silence; it was presence. Something old and enormous breathed here.

Kurt Gödel blinked. One moment he'd been in Princeton, hunched over his desk, neck-deep in metaphysical puzzles. The next—this. Candles flickered. Incense hung in the air like a question unanswered. He reached out and touched a stone pillar.

Solid. Real.

"Are you a pilgrim?" asked a voice behind him, calm and rounded, like it had traveled through centuries to find him.

Gödel turned.

The man before him wore a black robe. His eyes were serene but searching, as if he was looking not at Gödel but through him.

"I . . . might be," Gödel replied, dazed. "Where am I?"

"In Canterbury," the man said with a smile. "A house of prayer. And thought."

Then he paused and added, "I am Anselm" (1033–1109).

Gödel's breath caught. "Anselm? The philosopher? The one who tried to prove God exists . . . through reason alone?"

Anselm nodded gently. "And you are Kurt Gödel."

"But how—?"

Anselm's eyes twinkled. "The mind, when opened to the eternal, recognizes its kin."

Figure 19. Anselm assuming the pallium in Canterbury Cathedral. Source: E. M. Wilmot-Buxton, *Anselm* (George G. Harrap & Company, 1915), 136 (public domain).

They walked together beneath high arches that seemed less built than breathed—as if the cathedral were a thought, spoken aloud in stone. The kind of place where reason knelt beside reverence.

"I've seen your work," Anselm said. "You took up where I left off. Trying to prove God's existence not with scripture or sensation but with logic—with the very bones of reality."

"I only refined what you began," Gödel replied. "I gave it a formal coat of paint, perhaps. But the longing behind it? That was yours."

Anselm stopped beside a weathered lectern, where an old Latin text lay open: *Confessions*, by Augustine.

He touched the page reverently. "*Credo ut intelligam*," he whispered. "I believe so that I might understand."

Gödel smiled. "Yes. Faith doesn't shut the door to reason. It opens it. It says, 'Come in. Let's talk.'"

They sat beneath a stained-glass window where the Lamb of God glowed in warm gold and red.

"You know," Anselm said, "when I first tried to reason my way to God, I started with an idea. Not a feeling. Not a story. An idea: that if we can imagine a being so perfect that nothing greater could possibly exist . . . then that being must exist. Because if it didn't, well, it wouldn't be the greatest, would it?"

Gödel nodded.

Anselm continued, "I followed the trail. I laid down stones for others to walk on. I started with a simple thought: that some qualities—like love, justice, or wisdom—are genuinely good. Not just to us. Not just culturally. But always. Everywhere."

Anselm tilted his head. "Goodness isn't just an opinion. It's built into the fabric of reality."

"Like math," Gödel said. "Two plus two equals four, not just in this world but in every possible one. In the same way, kindness is better than cruelty—not just to humans, but in principle. They're opposites. You can't call them both good. The goodness of one cancels the other."

"And this matters," Anselm said slowly, "because if goodness is objective, then we can build upon it. Like climbing stones toward something higher."

"Exactly," Gödel said. "And if a thing is truly good—if it's good in essence—then it's not just good here and now. It would be good anywhere. In any world. That's what it means for something to be necessarily good—it doesn't bend with the wind of culture or time."

Anselm's eyes sparkled. "Eternal forms. Plato would approve."

Gödel chuckled. "Indeed. Now imagine this: What if there was a being who possessed every one of these good qualities? Not just one or two, but all of them. Perfect love. Perfect knowledge. Perfect justice. Perfect beauty. Every virtue, without flaw."

Anselm nodded. "That's what I meant by 'that than which nothing greater can be conceived.' *The maximal being*.

"And here's the twist," Anselm continued. "If that kind of being is even possible—just possible—then it can't just maybe exist. *It must exist.* Because a being that necessarily exists is more perfect than one that only might exist. And since this perfect being contains all good things, including necessary existence . . . it must be real."

Gödel leaned forward, like a man hearing his own thoughts spoken back to him, but with a new harmony.

"You're saying," he murmured, "that once we admit the possibility of such a being, we're no longer talking about imagination. We're talking about reality."

"Yes," Anselm said. "We step from the realm of what could be into what must be. And we don't do it through faith alone—we do it by following reason to its natural end."

Gödel was quiet for a moment. Then he said, "But what if someone denies that goodness is real? What if they say it's all just illusion, preference, social trickery?"

Anselm shrugged. "Then the whole argument collapses. But so does any real morality. If cruelty isn't wrong, just unpopular—then we're lost. Our outrage at injustice would be nothing more than taste. Like liking strawberries more than spinach."

He paused. "But no one really believes that. Not when the cruelty is aimed at them."

Anselm paused and smiled grimly. "So, my wager is this: Either goodness is real, and God follows logically—or nothing means anything."

They sat in silence for a while, beneath the colored light.

Finally, Gödel spoke again, more gently. "For me, this isn't just abstract logic. It's metaphysical homesickness. The universe feels incomplete without God. Like a cathedral with no altar. Or a symphony that never resolves."

Anselm closed his eyes. "And your incompleteness theorems? They don't contradict this?"

"No," Gödel said softly. "They confirm it. They show that no system, no matter how clever, can account for all truths within itself. There's always something true that lies just beyond. So, if reason alone can't seal the deal—it doesn't mean God isn't there. It means our tools are limited. But still . . . they point."

A shaft of golden light filtered down and touched the stone at their feet.

Anselm smiled. "Then perhaps we are not just philosophers."

Gödel looked up. "No. We are musicians. Tuning our minds to the divine melody."

They rose and walked to the altar, footsteps echoing like quiet percussion in the great cathedral. The building seemed to lift around them, not merely as stone, but as a symbol.

They knelt.

Under the Lamb of God's steady gaze, beneath vaults carved in sacred geometry, they were no longer bound by time.

Only wonder.

Anselm whispered again, *"I believe, so that I might understand."*

CHAPTER NINETEEN

THE MIRROR AND THE MAZE

— Gödel

Either mathematics is too big for the human mind, or the human mind is more than a machine.

—KURT GÖDEL

Kurt Gödel sat alone in his study, the faint glow of the lamp casting long shadows across his desk. Around him lay remnants of thoughts and dreams—sketches of impossible staircases, worn copies of philosophical treatises, notes on the nature of infinity, fragments of music, all gathered like puzzle pieces from some unreachable whole. Each encounter still lingered in his mind: Bach's endless fugues, Fibonacci's spiraling numbers, Mandelbrot's fractals, Kant's limits of reason, Lewis's unwavering logic of faith, Escher's impossible geometries. Each had left an imprint, an echo. Each had pulled him closer to some unseen, unprovable, undeniable truth.

And now, in the stillness, he found himself alone with the most difficult conversation of all: *the one with himself.*

Figure 20. Portrait of Kurt Gödel, one of the most significant logicians of the twentieth century, as a student in Vienna (between 1924 and 1927). Source: unknown author (public domain).

He stood, before walking slowly to the window. Outside, the night stretched wide and silent, the stars scattered like distant proofs in an equation too vast to comprehend. He pressed his hand against the cold glass, feeling the chill seep into his skin.

"What have I learned?" he asked the darkness, though he knew the question was meant for himself.

He closed his eyes, and the memories came. Again and again, he revisited and reasoned about his prior thoughts in search of conclusions—what does it all mean? The spirals of Fibonacci, unfolding in nature with a grace that defied mere chance. The paradoxes of Mandelbrot, revealing that infinity was not far but near, at the edges of every coastline, every cloud. The logic of Escher, folding worlds within worlds, structures that seemed impossible yet obeyed their own perfect order. The reasoned faith of Lewis, the disciplined humility of Kant, each man reaching for something beyond the mind's grasp.

Gödel's heart stirred with a thought he had long resisted, a whisper that had lingered just beyond his reasoning, waiting for this moment:

The fear of the Lord is the beginning of wisdom.

The old axiom echoed in his mind, ancient and sharp, as if it had been waiting for him all along.

He had tried so hard to approach the truth with logic, with proofs, with systems. Yet every path had led him back to the same conclusion: that reason could only go so far. That beyond the boundary of logic, there was something more. Something greater. Something *personal*.

He turned back to his desk, his eyes falling upon a Bible that lay half forgotten among his notes. Slowly, reverently, he opened it. His fingers traced the words of Proverbs, their simplicity burning with undeniable clarity:

For the Lord gives wisdom; from His mouth come knowledge and understanding (Proverbs 2:6).

It struck him deeply. The source of wisdom was not the mind. Not the world. Not the towering structures of logic and mathematics he had spent his life exploring. No—the source of wisdom was *from above*, from outside the system. And not from an abstract force but from a person. From a mind that was not impersonal but infinite and intimate.

"If the universe has order," Gödel whispered to himself, "if it follows patterns, if logic and beauty and music all obey something greater, then the source of that order must also be greater. Not just in magnitude but in being."

He paused, his breath catching. "And if that order leads to wisdom, then wisdom itself must have a source. Not in equations, not in proofs, but in a person. Because only a personal source can give wisdom. Only a mind can teach another mind."

The thought felt heavy, inevitable, as though it had always been the answer, waiting for him to stop resisting.

"It must be personal," he said again, softer now. "If truth were impersonal, how could we know it? How could we recognize it? How could we trust it? But if the truth is personal, if it is born of a mind—of *the* mind—then we recognize it because we are its reflection. We were made for it. And it . . . it seeks us."

He reached for his notebook and flipped back through pages of half-finished proofs, symbols that reached for the infinite but never quite grasped it.

"I have searched for completeness," he murmured, his eyes tracing the lines of his own theorems. "But completeness was never something to be proven. It is *something to be known*. To be loved."

And the words of the Psalmist came, ancient and eternal:

The fear of the Lord is the beginning of wisdom; all those who practice it have a good understanding (Psalm 111:10).

Gödel's heart ached with the simplicity of it. The fear of God, not terror but awe. Reverence. The recognition that there is something greater, something infinitely wise and personal, and that to stand before it is to know oneself as small, finite, incomplete.

But also loved. Also known.

If truth is personal, and the source of life and logic is a person, then that person must know those who seek him. Must desire to be known.

Gödel's hand trembled slightly as he reached for his pen, writing one final line beneath his theorems:

Truth is not a concept. It is a person.

And in that moment, the impossibilities seemed to resolve. The infinite spirals, the unreachable truths, and the limits of reason were not barriers but invitations. Invitations to know the one who had written those patterns into the fabric of the universe. The one who had placed eternity in man's heart, though man could not fully fathom it.

His eyes drifted to the sketch Escher had shown him in that strange, impossible gallery—the *Drawing Hands*, each hand sketching the other into existence, an endless act of creation and invitation. And now, Gödel saw it differently. It was not just a clever play on paradox but a reflection of the very nature of truth itself. The hand that draws is also the hand that reaches, as though inviting—or refusing to let go of—the one who searches. Perhaps this, too, was the nature of God: always reaching, always drawing the seeker closer, refusing to release those who long for what lies beyond reason. The infinite hand shapes the finite, while the finite longs to trace the infinite.

And perhaps that was the final beauty of it: that the infinite chose to be known.

Gödel sat back, his heart still and full. He realized that his journey had never been about proving God or proving the truth. It had been about meeting the one who had written the very patterns he spent his life chasing.

And in that, he found peace.

Logic could only take him so far. Wonder could only open the door. But wisdom . . . wisdom came from above. And wisdom, he now saw, was a hand extended in invitation—an invitation from the infinite, from the personal, from the one who is the source of life, truth, and all understanding.

And Gödel was ready to step through the door for the first time in his life.

CHAPTER TWENTY

FINDING WISDOM

—King Solomon

The fear of the Lord is the beginning of wisdom.

—PROVERBS 9:10

There are questions so ancient they echo in the soul before the mind can form them. They rise not from curiosity but from longing—from the ache that even the most brilliant discoveries cannot silence. One such question stirred again in the heart of a king.

King Solomon (970–931 BC) had done everything a man could do to find wisdom. He had ruled a kingdom, judged with brilliance, constructed marvels, written proverbs, pursued pleasures, and secured wealth beyond imagining. He had tasted every fruit the world offered and found each one to dissolve like mist in his mouth. Now, in the twilight of his life, he wandered the great temple—the house he had built not merely with stone and gold but with a longing for something eternal. The weight of his own words, penned in weariness and wonder, echoed in his heart: "Vanity of vanities . . . all is vanity."

He pondered the ones who would come after. Would they break through the futility he had uncovered? Would there be minds greater than his—minds that would solve the riddles he could only name? Or would their knowledge, however advanced, still be unable to grasp the thing that eluded him?

Far ahead in the long corridor of time, Kurt Gödel sat in his quiet Princeton study, surrounded not by scrolls or courts but by the absolute stillness of thought. The great logician had peered into the very structure of reason and found a fracture at its heart. Through the precision of symbols and proof, he had proven that no system of logic—no matter how complete—could explain itself entirely. Every formal structure left something outside, some truth it could not touch. Truth existed, but man's scaffolding could not reach it. And now, as the afternoon light passed across his desk, he found himself asking: Has anyone in history ever known this before me—not by theorem, but by life?

He was not thinking of the usual titans—not the Greeks with their dialogues, not the Enlightenment with its doubt—but someone deeper in the past. Someone who had stood at the pinnacle of human understanding and declared not triumph but futility. Gödel thought of the king who had said, "He has made everything beautiful in its time. Also, he has put eternity into man's heart, yet so that he cannot find out what God has done from the beginning to the end" (Ecclesiastes 3:11).

It was in that moment—through a tear in time and thought—that Solomon's yearning and Gödel's questions touched. And in that touch, the veil between ages was drawn back.

Gödel found himself no longer in his study but standing in a hall so magnificent that even the word *magnificent* felt thin. The architecture was not merely beautiful—it was otherworldly. Columns rose like a living flame, carved of cedar yet glowing as if lit from within. The gold that lined the walls shimmered, not with extravagance but with glory. There was an order to every curve and symmetry that defied human proportion, as if the angles themselves had been borrowed from eternity. It was unlike any place he had ever seen, not even the grandest cathedrals of Europe or Vitruvius's Rome. Those inspired awe. This inspired worship.

Figure 21. Illustration of King Solomon in old age (1 Kings 4:29–34). Source: Paul Gustave Louis Christophe Doré's English Bible (1866).

The Temple breathed the beauty of another world—not man-made but God-breathed, as though each beam had been carved with infinity in mind. Here, beauty was not ornamentation; it was revelation.

Across the chamber stood Solomon. Aged, robed, and calm—not diminished by time but distilled by it. His gaze, when it met Gödel's, needed no introduction. There was no surprise in him—only recognition.

They stood facing each other, two men divided by millennia yet bound by the same pursuit. Neither moved to speak at first, for the temple itself seemed to hold its breath.

It was Solomon who had first grown weary with the world. Not because he had failed to understand it but because he had understood it too well. He had known riches, laughter, dominion, and wisdom. But wisdom, for him, had not been the accumulation of facts or mastery of technique. It was something vertical—something that descended from above, not something that could be built from below. He had seen how knowledge spread wide, like a river, but wisdom fell like rain. The former could be measured and mapped. The latter could only be received.

And Gödel had come, centuries later, to a similar edge. With symbols and proofs, he had shown that no human effort, no accumulation of facts or reasoning, could close the circle. Every map had margins. Every system needed something beyond itself to make sense. He had discovered that knowledge, however vast, had an end—and at that end was either despair or divinity.

At first, they walked the temple together in silence, neither as master nor disciple. Each had something the other needed. Gödel had uncovered a flaw in the very fabric of human reason and wondered if it was a crack or a clue. Solomon had tasted every fruit under the sun and declared it empty unless touched by the sun above.

And then they spoke—not in argument, not in defense, but in the gentle offering of men who shared the same wound.

Solomon told of his endless striving, of how wisdom apart from God had only multiplied sorrow. That is what men call experience, cleverness, and brilliance—all of it turns to vapor when divorced from the one who gives meaning. "Wisdom," he said, "is not born of life's lessons. It is not the end of the study. It is the beginning of fear—holy fear—the awe of knowing there is one greater than the mind itself."

Gödel shared how even in the purest of human endeavors—mathematics—the pursuit of certainty had failed. Every system collapsed inward, and it needed an anchor that it could not generate. But he had never doubted that the truth existed. Only that man could arrive at it unaided. "It was never that I believed the universe was meaningless," he whispered, "only that meaning could not be found within the universe alone."

They paused before the veil—the entrance to the Holy of Holies. It stood not as a barrier but as an invitation. A symbol that truth dwelt somewhere just beyond reason's reach. Not lost—just hidden. Not invented—*revealed.*

Solomon stood with his hands folded, eyes resting on the golden fabric, heavy with centuries of meaning. "Wisdom," he said, "is not found in the accumulation of years, nor even in the brilliance of the mind. It is not the reward of effort but the gift of reverence. It descends, never ascends."

Gödel's brow furrowed slightly. "Then all our striving—science, mathematics, logic—it does not elevate us?"

Solomon turned slowly toward him. "It may illuminate. But it does not complete. Knowledge spreads wide, yes—like a great plain, endlessly measurable. But wisdom falls like rain from above. Vertical, not horizontal."

Gödel nodded slowly, as if something were settling into place. "That's what I felt in my work. That no matter how elegant the structure, it required something beyond itself to make sense of it."

"And you named that structure's limit," Solomon said, "and in doing so, you pointed beyond it."

Gödel looked up at the towering veil. "Sometimes I wonder if my theorems were not so much discoveries as confessions. A mathematician admitting that reason, though sharp and luminous, cannot close the circle."

Solomon smiled faintly. "Then you are wiser than most. I wrote of vanity, not to despair, but to expose the futility of finding meaning under the sun. All must be measured in light of the one who reigns above it."

Gödel stepped forward and said, his voice lower now, more personal, "Do you believe, then, that the limits of understanding were given to us—intentionally?"

"Yes," Solomon said. "As a mercy. To drive the proud to humility, and the seeker to worship. For what man can boast of knowing when he cannot even make sense of his own heart?"

Gödel hesitated, then confessed, "All my life, I believed that truth existed. I trusted in reason because I believed in something greater than reason—something that made it possible."

Solomon's eyes softened. "Then you believed rightly."

There was a long pause. The temple grew quieter still, as if every stone listened.

Gödel spoke again. "I have always felt that the universe, left to itself, would be absurd. Not chaotic, necessarily—but insufficient. As though someone had built a great cathedral and left the altar empty."

"Yet it is not empty," Solomon said. "Only veiled. Like the Holy of Holies."

Gödel stepped closer to the curtain. "I used to think logic might lift that veil. That if I were careful enough, thorough enough, the structure of reality would resolve. But all it ever did was remind me that I am not the Creator."

"And that," Solomon said, "is the beginning of wisdom."

A silence passed between them that needed no words.

Then Solomon said, almost gently, "You know, I once asked: What does man gain by all the toil at which he toils under the sun? And I found no answer—until I realized the question itself was malformed. Because man was never meant to toil for gain but to live in fear of God and keep his commandments. That is the whole duty of man."

Gödel exhaled, as though releasing a lifetime of tension. "Then my theorems were not a failure."

"They were an *invitation*," Solomon replied. "A summons to look up."

Gödel turned his face toward the sacred veil. "And now I believe more than ever that God exists. Not because I can prove him, but because without him, nothing else can be proven."

Solomon nodded slowly. "Then we have both come to the edge of reason—and beyond it, found reverence."

CHAPTER TWENTY-ONE

THE FINAL WORD

— Christ

Blessed are those who have not seen and yet have believed.

—JOHN 20:29

Kurt Gödel had encountered many great minds in his journeys through thought—Socrates, Aristotle, Pascal, Fibonacci, Kant, and Popper. But now, as he stood beneath the vast, star-filled sky, he felt something different. Something beyond philosophy, beyond mathematics.

He did not know where he was, only that it was neither the past nor the future. The air was still, yet alive. The night sky stretched above him, deeper than any theorem could explain, more infinite than any number. And standing before him, radiant yet humble, was the man Gödel had spent his life trying to understand without realizing it.

Jesus Christ.

Gödel, usually precise in his words, found himself stumbling. "I . . . I do not know how this is possible. I do not know what to say."

Jesus smiled with kindness and depth in his eyes, which Gödel had never seen in any thinker before. "Then ask, Gödel. You have always asked. That is why you are here."

THE NATURE OF TRUTH

Gödel steadied himself, gathering his mind. His eyes shed the hint of a sparkling tear. "I have spent my life proving that truth is incomplete. That no system of logic can contain all truths within itself. That knowledge always leaves something outside, something unprovable but undeniably real. But you . . . you claim to be the truth itself. How is that possible?"

Jesus nodded. "You have seen the limits of knowledge, Kurt. You have seen that even mathematics, the most structured of human endeavors, cannot explain everything. But the truth is not confined to proofs. Truth cannot be contained in a system—it is something greater. It is living."

Gödel frowned, his mind racing. "But logic, reason—these are the tools we use to understand the universe. If we abandon them, are we not left with blind belief?"

Jesus's expression remained calm. "I do not ask you to abandon reason. I gave you reason. But reason alone cannot lead you to the fullness of truth. You have seen it yourself—every system of knowledge is incomplete. Every attempt to define reality through human logic alone fails in the face of something greater. And yet, even knowing this, men still place their faith in their own minds rather than in what is beyond them."

THE NECESSITY OF UNCERTAINTY

Gödel's breath was steady, but he felt something stirring within him—a realization he had not yet fully grasped. "Then why, Lord?

Why did you create a world where knowledge is incomplete? Why allow uncertainty at all?"

Jesus's gaze did not waver. "Because *certainty removes choice*. If I made my existence undeniable, if I left no room for doubt, then there would be no true faith. *Faith must be chosen*. Love must be chosen. If I forced belief, it would not be belief at all—it would be mere recognition, like acknowledging the sun in the sky. But I desire something more than mere acknowledgment. I desire love, and love must be freely given."

Gödel felt his heart pound. "So, the very structure of knowledge, the very incompleteness I discovered—it was meant to be this way? It was part of your design?"

Jesus nodded. "It was necessary. If man could prove my existence as he proves a theorem, where would be the choice to trust, to seek, to love? And yet, I have not left men without evidence. The heavens declare my glory. The laws of physics, the beauty of mathematics, the moral law written in every heart—these are my fingerprints. But to see them, man must choose to see."

THE FAITH IN MAN OR GOD

Gödel took a deep breath. "But what of those who put their faith in reason alone? In science? In human understanding?"

Jesus sighed, not in weariness but in deep sorrow. "To have faith in man's knowledge alone is to build on shifting sand. Science and reason are gifts, but not the foundation of truth. They can illuminate, but they cannot save. A man who builds his house on reason alone will find it crumble when reason reaches its limits. But a man who builds on truth—on me—will stand when all else fails."

Gödel's mind reeled. He had spent his life proving the limits of knowledge, showing that no human system could hold all truth.

And yet, here was the answer he had never considered. It was not that truth did not exist—it was that truth was beyond man's reach through logic alone.

"Then you have given us the choice," Gödel said slowly. "To trust in what we can see, knowing it is incomplete. Or to trust in you, whom we cannot see but who is complete."

Jesus nodded. "Yes. And the consequences of that choice are real. Justice demands that those who reject the truth must face the absence of it. In the end, those who build their lives around themselves will find that they have built nothing at all. But those who seek me, even through their doubt, will find that I have been seeking them all along."

THE CLOSING OF ALL THINGS

Gödel looked up at the sky, at the infinite stretch of stars. He had always known that human understanding was limited, but only now did he understand why. His throat tightened, a fragile dam against the flood of emotion, as tears welled and spilled—silent, shimmering proof of a heart finally understood.

"Then all things must come to a close," he murmured. "Knowledge will fail. Systems will collapse. But the truth—you—remain."

Jesus stepped forward, placing a hand on Gödel's shoulder. "Yes. And in the end, all things will be made clear. The limits will be removed. Those who have chosen truth will see me as I am. And those who have built on themselves will see what they have lost."

Gödel felt a weight lifted from him—not a burden removed but an understanding granted. "Then I will write. I will speak. I will tell them that the search for truth is not in vain, but that it must lead to you."

Figure 22. Wood engraving of the crucifixion of Jesus (1866) by Gustave Doré.

Jesus smiled. "Then go, my friend. You have seen. Now help others to see. Yet, remember, all choose freely—*nobody is without excuse*. Help them see and understand."

And with that, the vision faded. The stars remained. The knowledge remained.

But now, Gödel understood. And that made all the difference.

EPILOGUE

BEYOND THE AXIOMS

The more I reflect on the problem, the more I become convinced that it has much less to do with mathematics than with philosophy and even theology.

—SAMUEL E. NAVARRO

WE'VE TRAVELED THROUGH A LABYRINTH.

From the quiet corridors of mathematics to the aching wonder of art, from the limits of logic to the questions that logic cannot touch. We've sat with saints and skeptics, physicists and poets. We've watched Gödel listen, argue, tremble, and finally—kneel.

If you've come this far, maybe something inside you is trembling too.

Maybe you've realized that the most powerful truths in life are not the ones you can prove, but the ones you must *choose*. The ones that are lived long before they are understood. The ones that feel, at first, like questions—and turn out, in the end, to be invitations.

You don't have to be a logician to feel the pull of Gödel's theorems. All of us live inside systems—families, cultures, schools of thought, institutions, and unspoken assumptions. All of us inherit the axioms of our age. But what happens when those systems fail to explain the ache in our chest? What happens when we come face to face with something true that we can't derive from anything else?

That's where this book lives.

Somewhere between music and math. Between proof and poetry. Between the mind's sharp edge and the soul's quiet hunger.

It's tempting to think that if we could just figure everything out, we'd finally be free. But maybe it's the other way around. Maybe freedom begins when we admit what we can't figure out—and walk forward anyway. Not blindly. But humbly. Eyes wide open.

Maybe the final leap is not into reason but into love.

Maybe the truth is not a theorem but a person.

Gödel's journey doesn't really end here. And neither does yours.

Because if the limits of logic brought us here, then paradox is what waits on the other side.

Sometimes, we need to face the unsolvable—and *choose* anyway, *wisely*. To wrestle with Zeno's stillness, Buridan's indecision, and Russell's contradiction.

To step into the spaces where reason fails, not with despair, but with courage.

But that's another path. Another flame to follow through the fog.

This book closes. But the door that opened remains ajar.

So, if your heart is still burning, if the questions still hum under your breath, keep walking. Keep asking. Keep choosing the better mystery. And when the silence returns—as it always does—listen for the music that logic can't write.

Because some things are too beautiful to be proven.

And that's the point.

WHY GÖDEL?

In choosing Kurt Gödel as the protagonist of this exploration, I sought a voice that embodies both the pinnacle of logical rigor and the profound mystery that lies at the edge of human understanding. No other figure in twentieth-century thought so clearly demonstrates how our most cherished systems of knowledge—mathematics and formal logic—carry within them an inherent boundary. Gödel was not merely a brilliant logician; he was a thinker whose life and work invite us to confront *the humility required of every serious inquirer.*

Gödel connected mathematics deeply with philosophy and metaphysics and explored theological implications, especially through his ontological proof of God.

By placing him at the center of this book, I hope to leverage his intellectual authority to lead readers beyond familiar debates and into the territory where certainty gives way to wonder.

WHY THE INCOMPLETENESS THEOREMS?

Gödel's two incompleteness theorems, first published in 1931, reveal an unsettling truth: Any consistent axiomatic system capable of expressing elementary arithmetic must contain statements that are true yet unprovable within that very system. In effect, these theorems demonstrate that completeness and consistency cannot coexist in any sufficiently rich formal theory. Mathematics—long regarded as the archetype of infallible knowledge—turns out to be subject to an inescapable horizon of unresolvable questions. The implications ripple outward: If our most exacting discipline admits its own limits, then every other field of study, from philosophy to biology, must reckon with its own forms of incompleteness.

THE END

The fear of the Lord is the beginning of knowledge, but fools despise wisdom and instruction.

—PROVERBS 1:7

BIBLIOGRAPHY AND SOURCES

FOR *GÖDEL AND THE INCOMPLETE PROOF*

PART I lists works that appear in multiple chapters (principal sources). Part II lists chapter-specific citations; a source is omitted from a chapter if it is already listed in Part I and no page-specific reference is given. Non-English titles include an English translation in brackets.

PART I: PRINCIPAL SOURCES

- Bertrand Russell and Alfred North Whitehead, *Principia Mathematica* (1910–13). Evoked as the emblem of humankind's dream to enclose all truth in logic, which Gödel's incompleteness theorems later "cracked."
- Kurt Gödel, "On Formally Undecidable Propositions of Principia Mathematica and Related Systems I" (1931). Gödel's first incompleteness theorem, demonstrating that any sufficiently expressive formal system contains true statements that cannot be proven within the system itself—mirroring the necessity of stepping beyond reason to embrace living truth.

- Stephen Budiansky, *Journey to the Edge of Reason: The Life of Kurt Gödel* (2021).
- John D. Barrow, *Impossibility, The Limits of Science and the Science of Limits* (1998).
- Douglas R. Hofstatdter, *Gödel, Escher, Bach: An Eternal Golden Braid* [also known as GEB] (1979). Explores deep parallels between Bach's recursive musical structures, Gödel's logical constructions, and Escher's visual paradoxes.

PART II: CHAPTER-SPECIFIC CITATIONS

CHAPTER 1: THE MACHINE THAT COULDN'T KNOW—VON NEUMANN

- David Hilbert, "Hilbert's Program" (1900 Paris address) and related publications. The formal axiomatic initiative aiming for completeness and consistency in math.
- Logical Positivism (Vienna Circle). Philosophical movement (Rudolf Carnap, Otto Neurath, etc.) stressing that meaningful statements must be logically or empirically verifiable.
- John von Neumann and Oskar Morgenstern, *Theory of Games and Economic Behavior* (1944). Foundation of modern game theory, referenced in relation to Von Neumann's polymath genius.
- John F. Nash, Jr., "Non-Cooperative Games" (PhD thesis, 1950). Nash's equilibrium refinement, noted as building on Von Neumann's game-theoretic groundwork.
- Albert Einstein and Kurt Gödel, Institute for Advanced Study companionship biographical accounts of their famed walks and conversations at Princeton (*When Einstein Walked with Gödel: Excursions to the Edge of Thought* by Jim Holt; *A World Without Time: The Forgotten Legacy of Gödel and Einstein* by Pale Yourgrau; *Time Bandits*, article in the *New Yorker* by Jim Holt).
- Kurt Gödel's ontological proof (manuscript published posthumously in 1987 in *Collected Works*). Gödel's formal, mathematically framed version of the ontological argument for God's existence. He first drafted the argument around 1941 but did not reveal it, possibly apart from Einstein, until 1970 when he circulated it among a few close friends.
- Hao Wang, *Reflections on Kurt Gödel* (1987).
- Norman Macrae, *John von Neumann: The Scientific Genius Who Pioneered the Modern Computer, Game Theory, Nuclear Deterrence, and Much More* (1992).
- A. J. Ayer, *Language, Truth and Logic* (1936). Classic Vienna Circle manifesto.

CHAPTER 2: TRUTH ON TRIAL—POPPER

- Karl Popper, *The Logic of Scientific Discovery* (1934 German; 1959 Eng.). Introduces the principle of falsification, arguing that scientific theories progress by refutation rather than verification. Popper's demarcation examples contrasting unfalsifiable fields (astrology, psychoanalysis) with empirically testable sciences (evolutionary biology, physics).
- Alan Turing, "On Computable Numbers, with an Application to the Decision Problem" (1936). Establishes the halting problem, showing there is no general algorithm to decide whether arbitrary programs halt.
- Kurt Gödel's ontological proof (manuscript, posthumously published in his *Collected Works*). Gödel's own formal argument for the necessary existence of God, reflecting his theistic leanings.
- Archimedes, *On Floating Bodies* (ca. 250 BC). Source of the buoyancy analogy: A body "sinks until it finds the density that bears it."
- Karl Popper, *Unended Quest: An Intellectual Biography* (1976).

CHAPTER 3: THE UNCERTAINTY OF KNOWING—SCHRÖDINGER

- Erwin Schrödinger, "I have no doubt that the universe is governed by laws, but these laws may still be incomplete." Paraphrased from Schrödinger's published reflections on the limits of physical law (cf. "What Is Life?" lectures, 1944).
- Erwin Schrödinger, "The Present Situation in Quantum Mechanics" (1935). Original paper introducing the "Schrödinger's cat" thought experiment to illustrate quantum superposition.
- Albert Einstein, "God does not play dice." Famous retort to quantum indeterminacy, from his correspondence with Max Born (letter, December 1926).
- Alan M. Turing, "On Computable Numbers, with an Application to the Decision Problem" (1936). Establishes the halting problem and the fundamental limits of algorithmic computation.
- Richard Feynman, "Simulating Physics with Computers" (1981). Seminal lecture proposing the use of quantum systems to perform computations beyond classical reach (early quantum computing concept).
- Zeno of Elea, "Paradoxes" (ca. 5th century BC). The paradoxes of motion (e.g., Achilles and the tortoise) illustrate horizons that retreat as you approach—analogous to Gödel's moving boundary of provability.
- John Gribbin, *In Search of Schrödinger's Cat: Quantum Physics and Reality* (1984).

- Walter Moore, *Schrödinger: Life and Thought* (1989).
- Paul A. M. Dirac, *The Principles of Quantum Mechanics* (1930).

CHAPTER 4: THE HIDDEN SEQUENCE—FIBONACCI

- Leonardo of Pisa (Fibonacci), *Liber Abaci* (1202). Introduces the rabbit-pair thought experiment and the sequence 1, 1, 2, 3, 5, 8 ... on which the chapter is centered.
- Leonardo da Vinci, *Vitruvian Man* (ca. 1490).
- Leonardo da Vinci, *The Last Supper* (ca. 1495–98).
- Keith Devlin, *The Man of Numbers: Fibonacci's Arithmetic Revolution* (2011). A modern biography of Fibonacci that places *Liber Abaci* in its historical context.
- Mario Livio, *The Golden Ratio: The Story of Phi, the World's Most Astonishing Number* (2002). Explores the mathematics, history, and cultural impact of ϕ, with many natural-pattern examples.
- Ian Stewart, *Nature's Numbers: The Unreal Reality of Mathematics* (1995). Examines how mathematical sequences—including Fibonacci's—arise in biology, physics, and beyond.
- C. Martin Gardner, "Fibonacci's Rabbits Revisited," *Scientific American* (1974). A classic exposition of the original rabbit problem and its surprising generalizations.
- Robin Wilson, *Mathematics and the Search for Knowledge* (1984). Places medieval mathematics—Fibonacci included—within the broader sweep of mathematical history.

CHAPTER 5: FRACTALS AND THE FACE OF CHAOS—MANDELBROT

- Benoît Mandelbrot, "Chaos is not the absence of order, but the presence of hidden patterns." Paraphrased from Mandelbrot's reflections on fractal geometry and chaos in *The Fractal Geometry of Nature* (1982).
- Benoît Mandelbrot, *The Fractal Geometry of Nature* (1982). Introduces the concept of self-similarity, roughness, and the formal definition of fractals (e.g., the Mandelbrot set).
- Benoît Mandelbrot, "How Long Is the Coast of Britain? Statistical Self-Similarity and Fractional Dimension," *Science* 156 (1967): 636–38. Landmark paper showing that natural coastlines exhibit fractal (scale-invariant) behavior.
- Benoît B. Mandelbrot, *The (Mis)Behavior of Markets: A Fractal View of Risk,*

Ruin, and Reward (2004). Applies fractal concepts to financial markets—showing how Mandelbrot's ideas revolutionized risk analysis.

- Fred Wolf, *The Beauty of Fractals* (1986). A richly illustrated survey of fractal art and the mathematics behind it.

CHAPTER 6: IRREDUCIBLE COMPLEXITY—C. D. BROAD

- C. D. Broad, "Induction is the glory of science and the scandal of philosophy." From Broad's discussion of the paradoxes of induction in *Induction, Probability, and Inference* (1926).
- C. D. Broad, *The Mind and Its Place in Nature* (1925). Lays out his strong emergentist view that new, irreducible properties (like consciousness) can arise from but not be reduced to physical substrates.
- Michael J. Behe, *Darwin's Black Box: The Biochemical Challenge to Evolution* (1996). Introduces the concept of irreducible complexity, arguing that specific biological systems cannot be built up by successive, slight modifications.
- Charles Darwin, *On the Origin of Species* (1859). Darwin's proviso that if any complex organ could not be shown to arise via "numerous, successive, slight modifications," his theory would break down.
- C. D. Broad, *Scientific Thought* (1937). Further essays on the limits of scientific explanation and the role of metaphysics.
- Thomas Nagel, "What Is It Like to Be a Bat?" (1974). A classic articulation of the "hard problem" of consciousness and subjective experience.
- David J. Chalmers, *The Conscious Mind: In Search of a Fundamental Theory* (1996). Develops the distinction between the "easy" and "hard" problems of consciousness, defending a form of property dualism. A collection exploring different models of emergence across disciplines.

CHAPTER 7: THE FUGUE OF INFINITY—BACH

- Johann Sebastian Bach. *The Musical Offering* (1747). The set of canons and fugues Bach composed for Frederick the Great, famous for its intricate contrapuntal puzzles.
- Christoph Wolff, *Johann Sebastian Bach: The Learned Musician* (2000). A comprehensive modern biography situating Bach's contrapuntal mastery in both his life and the broader intellectual currents of the Baroque.
- Derek B. Scott, *Bach and the Patterns of Invention* (1985). An in-depth study of Bach's canons and fugues, analyzing their mathematical and structural ingenuity.

- John Butt, *Bach's Dialogue with Modernity: Perspectives on the Passions* (2010). Discusses how Bach's works anticipate modern ideas of structure, tension, and resolution—useful for drawing connections to Gödelian themes.

CHAPTER 8: HANDS THAT DRAW THEMSELVES—ESCHER

- M. C. Escher, *Drawing Hands* (1948 lithograph). The self-referential image of two hands drawing each other that sparks Gödel's reflection on loops and external perspective.
- Maurits Cornelis Escher biographical details. Born in 1898 in Leeuwarden, Netherlands; formative sketches of Moorish tessellations at the Alhambra and Romanesque cloisters of Italy (see Escher's sketchbooks and letters) reflect his early immersion in geometric patterns.
- M. C. Escher, *Relativity* (1953 lithograph). Depicts impossible staircases and multiple gravity frames—used in the chapter to illustrate incompatible yet internally consistent systems.
- M. C. Escher, *Ascending and Descending* (1960 lithograph). The perpetual staircase, another visualization of paradoxical recursion mentioned as part of Escher's fascination with infinite loops.
- M. C. Escher, *Metamorphosis* series (1937–60). Fish-turning-into-birds transformations illustrating continuous change within a single bounded form (alluded to when Escher spreads his sketches).

CHAPTER 9: THE ETERNAL PROPORTIONS—VITRUVIUS

- Marcus Vitruvius Pollio, *De Architectura* [Ten Books on Architecture] (ca. 15 BC). Vitruvius's foundational treatise on Roman engineering, aesthetics, and the "harmonious proportions" of buildings, mirroring the human body.
- Leon Battista Alberti, *De Pictura* [On Painting] (1435). Introduced the principles of linear perspective and codified the application of mathematical proportion to visual art, directly inspired by Vitruvian symmetry.
- Andrea Palladio, *I quattro libri dell'architettura* [The Four Books of Architecture] (1570). Renaissance villas and palaces designed according to Vitruvian rules of harmony and balance, exemplifying the revival of classical proportions in built form.
- Leonardo da Vinci, *Vitruvian Man* (ca. 1490). Da Vinci's iconic drawing translates Vitruvius's "height equals arm span" into the archetype of human-centered proportion and the link between microcosm and macrocosm.

- Joseph Rykwert, *The First Moderns: The Architects of the Eighteenth Century* (1980). Explores how Vitruvian ideas were reinterpreted and transformed by neoclassical architects in the centuries following Palladio.

CHAPTER 10: SCIVIAS AND NEUMES—HILDEGARD VON BINGEN

- Hildegard von Bingen, *Scivias* [Know the Ways] (completed ca. 1151). Her illustrated theological treatise, featuring mandalas, visionary creatures, and the famous *frontispiece* of her receiving a divine vision.
- *Liber Vitae Meritorum* [Book of the Rewards of Life] (ca. 1158).
- *Liber Divinorum Operum* [Book of Divine Works] (ca. 1163).
- Hildegard's musical collection, *Symphonia Armonie Celestium Revelationum* [Symphony of the Harmony of Celestial Revelations] (ca. 1151–58).
- Emperor Frederick I "Barbarossa" (reigned 1155–90). Political backdrop of Hildegard's later life, including her letters of counsel to secular and ecclesiastical rulers. Sources: *Frederick Barbarossa: The Prince and the Myth*, by John B. Freed (1916); *Frederick Barbarossa: A Study in Medieval Politics*, Cornell University Press, 1069; *The Deeds of Frederick Barbarossa*, Otto of Freising and Rahewin, translated 2003 by Charles Christopher Mierow).

CHAPTER 11: THE DRIP OF INFINITY—JACKSON POLLOCK

- Art of This Century gallery (opened 1942). Peggy Guggenheim's seminal New York gallery that championed avant-garde artists, including Jackson Pollock. In 1943, Guggenheim discovered Pollock, gave him his first solo exhibition, and offered him a contract with the freedom to devote himself to painting. She sponsored three more solo shows for Pollock before the gallery's closing in 1947. For more, see: Guggenheim New York Museum (Guggenheim.org).
- Jackson Pollock's drip technique (ca. 1947). Pollock's innovation of laying canvases on the floor and splattering enamel paint, first widely exhibited in 1947 exhibitions at Peggy Guggenheim's gallery.
- Thomas Hart Benton (1889–1975). Pollock's instructor at the Art Students League of New York, whose regional-style murals contrasted with Pollock's later abstraction.
- "Jackson Pollock: Is He the Greatest Painter Alive in the United States?" *Life* (August 8, 1949). The profile that brought Pollock's work to mass attention and cemented his public identity.

- Richard P. Taylor et al., "Fractal Analysis of Pollock's Paintings," *Nature* 399: 422 (1999). Studies showing that Pollock's drip paintings exhibit fractal dimensions similar to naturally occurring patterns. The landmark paper quantifying the fractal characteristics in Pollock's canvases.

CHAPTER 12: THE DEATH OF CERTAINTY—SOCRATES

- Socrates, "The unexamined life is not worth living." From Plato's *Apology* (ca. 399 BC). Socrates's defense at his trial, asserting the necessity of continual self-examination.
- Socratic method. The dialectical technique of cooperative questioning and refutation, as depicted in Plato's early dialogues.
- Socrates's imprisonment and execution by hemlock (399 BC). Historical account from Plato's *Phaedo*, describing Socrates's calm acceptance of death rather than renouncing his philosophy.
- Aristotle's epistemology. Referenced indirectly in Aristotle's *Posterior Analytics* (ca. 350 BC) when Socrates's method is contrasted with Aristotle's more systematic approach to categorizing knowledge.

CHAPTER 13: THE WAGER OF THE HEART—PASCAL

- Blaise Pascal, "All of humanity's problems stem from man's inability to sit quietly in a room alone." From Pascal's *Pensées* [Thoughts] (posthumously published 1670), reflecting on human restlessness.
- Blaise Pascal, *Pensées*, "Pascal's Wager" (ca. 1670). The argument that, given infinite stakes, reason compels one to "bet" on God's existence.
- Leonardo Fibonacci, *Liber Abaci* (1202). Introduces the Fibonacci sequence (1, 1, 2, 3, 5 . . .) and the related golden ratio, here evoked as cosmic architecture.
- Golden ratio (ϕ). The limiting ratio of successive Fibonacci numbers, often observed in nature and art.
- Steven Shapin, *Pascal's Wager: How the World's Greatest Thinkers Have Reasoned About Faith* (2008). Surveys the historical debate around Pascal's wager and its influence on philosophy and theology.

CHAPTER 14: REASON'S EDGE—KANT

- Immanuel Kant, *Critique of Pure Reason* (1781, 2nd ed. 1787). Kant's foundational work arguing that human knowledge is limited to phenomena (appearances) and that noumena (things in themselves) are unknowable—"I had to deny knowledge in order to make room for faith."

- René Descartes, *Meditations on First Philosophy* (1641). Source of Cartesian methodological skepticism and the "evil demon" thought experiment.
- David Hume, *An Enquiry Concerning Human Understanding* (1748). Hume's acute empiricist skepticism about induction and causality.
- Immanuel Kant, *Critique of Practical Reason* (1788). Introduces the moral "postulates" (God, freedom, immortality) and the famous pair of "the starry heavens above me and the moral law within me."

CHAPTER 15: FREEDOM'S RECKONING—SARTRE

- Bertrand Russell and Alfred North Whitehead, *Principia Mathematica* (1910–13). Symbol of the dream to ground all truth in formal logic—subsequently "cracked" by Gödel's incompleteness theorems.
- Jean-Paul Sartre, *La Nausée* [Nausea] (1938). Sartre's novel articulating existential nausea and the absence of inherent meaning, featuring Antoine Roquentin's confrontation with contingency.
- Auschwitz-Birkenau (1940–45). The Nazi extermination camp, historical backdrop for testing existential freedom against systematic evil.
- Simone de Beauvoir. Sartre's lifelong companion, she witnessed his decline as he faced the realities of his own mortality in his final years. Their unique and unconventional intellectual and personal bond spanned over fifty years.
- Jean-Paul Sartre, *Being and Nothingness* (1943). His magnum opus setting out the ontology of freedom and the structures of consciousness.
- Elie Wiesel, *Night* (1956). A first-person account of the Holocaust's moral abyss and the challenge it poses to human freedom and faith.

CHAPTER 16: THE MEASURE OF A SOUL—FAUST

- Anonymous German author, *Historia von D. Johann Faustus* (1587) [*The History of the Damnable Life and Deserved Death of Doctor John Faustus*], English translation (1592). The first printed Faust chapbook by Johann Spies, which introduced the scholar-sorcerer legend and the pact with the devil.
- Johann Wolfgang von Goethe, *Faust: Der Tragödie erster Teil* [Faust Part I] (1808) and *Faust: Der Tragödie zweiter Teil* [Faust Part II] (1832). Goethe's two-part poetic drama that reimagines and elevates the Faust legend to its pinnacle in world literature.
- Blaise Pascal, "Pascal's Wager" from *Pensées* (ca. 1670). Alluded to

indirectly in Gödel's reflection on wagering one's soul—contrasted with Faust's fatal mis-bet.

- Christopher Marlowe, *Doctor Faustus* (ca. 1592). The Elizabethan tragedy that popularized Faust in English literature and explores the moral perils of overreaching ambition.
- Sigmund Freud, *Beyond the Pleasure Principle* (1920). Offers insight into the darker drives of human ambition and the self-destructive impulses that underlie many Faustian bargains.

CHAPTER 17: LONGING AND THE LOGOS—C. S. LEWIS

- C. S. Lewis, *Mere Christianity* (1952). Lewis's classic apologetic work, especially Book III's famous "desire argument": "If I find in myself a desire which no experience in this world can satisfy, the most probable explanation is that I was made for another world."
- C. S. Lewis, *The Great Divorce* (1945). His visionary tale of souls journeying from a gray town to a land of light, illustrating the necessity of becoming "real enough" to abide in a higher realm.
- C. S. Lewis, *The Screwtape Letters* (1942). The epistolary satire revealing how evil undermines truth not by logic but by distraction, half truths, and complacency.
- C. S. Lewis, *Surprised by Joy* (1955). The personal autobiography in which Lewis recounts his intellectual journey from atheism to Christianity, illuminating the interplay of reason and longing.

CHAPTER 18: A DIVINE AXIOM—ANSELM

- Anselm of Canterbury, *Proslogion* [Discourse on the Existence of God] (1077–78). Where Anselm formulates the ontological argument defining God as "that than which nothing greater can be conceived."
- Saint Augustine, *Confessions* (ca. 397–400). Source of the maxim "Credo ut intelligam" ["I believe so that I might understand"], quoted by Anselm as the posture of faith opening the door to understanding.
- Plato, *Republic* (ca. 380 BC). Alluded to when Anselm wittily observes, "Plato would approve" of the appeal to eternal forms underlying objective goodness.

CHAPTER 19: THE MIRROR AND THE MAZE—GÖDEL

- Kurt Gödel: "Either mathematics is too big for the human mind, or the human mind is more than a machine." Gödel's remark (often attributed to his 1951 Gibbs Lecture), capturing the paradox of human cognition versus formal systems.

- M. C. Escher, *Drawing Hands* (1948). The self-referential lithograph of two hands sketching each other, evoked here as a metaphor for the infinite invitation of truth.
- W.T. Richman, *Gödel's Proof: An Introduction to the Incompleteness Theorems* (2003). A clear, nontechnical walk through Gödel's original incompleteness results, ideal for understanding the limits of formal systems.
- James L. Crenshaw, *Psalms: An Introduction and Commentary* (1985). Provides historical and theological background on the wisdom literature of Proverbs and Psalms, clarifying the biblical texts Gödel encounters.

CHAPTER 20: FINDING WISDOM—KING SOLOMON

- "The fear of the Lord is the beginning of wisdom, and the knowledge of the Holy One is insight" (Prov. 9:10 [ESV]).
- "Vanity of vanities, says the Preacher, vanity of vanities! All is vanity" (Ecc. 1:2 [ESV]).
- "He has made everything beautiful in its time. Also, he has put eternity into the human heart, yet so that man will not find out what God has done from the beginning to the end" (Ecc. 3:11 [(ESV]).
- "The end of the matter; all has been heard. Fear God and keep his commandments, for this is the whole duty of man" (Ecc. 12:13 [ESV]).

CHAPTER 21: THE FINAL WORD—CHRIST

- "Jesus said to him, 'Have you believed because you have seen me? Blessed are those who have not seen and yet have believed'" (John 20:29 [ESV]).
- C. S. Lewis, *Miracles* (1947). Argues for the plausibility of divine action transcending natural systems—complementary to Gödel's insight that not all truth fits inside a formal frame.

EPILOGUE: BEYOND THE AXIOMS

- Zeno of Elea, Paradoxes (ca. 5th century BC). The famous paradoxes (Achilles and the tortoise, the arrow) illustrating the challenge of motion and division—symbols of limits within reason.
- Jean Buridan, *Sophismata* (14th century). Medieval discussions of the

"Buridan's ass" paradox, where a donkey placed equidistant between two equal bales of hay cannot rationally choose one—an emblem of indeterminate decision.

- Bertrand Russell, "Russell's Paradox" in *Principia Mathematica* (1910–13). The set-theoretic paradox showing that naive set comprehension leads to contradiction—another demonstration that some self-referential systems must fail.